WEAVING WORDS

A MEDLEY OF SHORT STORIES

BRENDA
BRINKLEY

Publishing Coordinator – Sharon Kizziah-Holmes
Cover Photo – Brenda Brinkley

Paperback-Press
an imprint of A & S Publishing
A & S Holmes, Inc.

ISBN -13: 978-1-951772-15-4

DEDICATION

To my husband Gary, who has always supported and encouraged my dreams. To our grown children, Patricia and Freddy, a constant source of joy.

CONTENTS

ACKNOWLEDGMENTS

Thanks be to God who makes all things possible.

Thank you to my mom who took me on countless trips to the bookmobile and fed my love of reading, and to my dad who always pushed me to do my best.

Thank you to Sharon Kizziah-Holmes for all her help putting this together, and to Shirley McCann for a great editing job.

Thank you to all the editors I have been privileged to work with over the years.

THE BIG TIPPER

The aroma of bacon sizzling on the grill mingled with the stench of cigarette smoke wafting from the back of the small café.

"Hey, Katie, can we get more coffee here?" Loud and proud, Luke Mason was the mouthpiece for the coffee crowd.

"Be right there, Luke." Katie grabbed the coffee pot.

"He'll be here for at least an hour. Somebody ought to put a lid on his bottomless cup." Lucy glared at Katie. "Do you always have to be so cheerful?"

With a nod and a smile, Katie whisked past Lucy and headed toward the table of men in the back. Steam rose as she filled the white cups waiting on the red-checkered tablecloth. The men had removed the plastic floral centerpiece and replaced it with an ash tray. It was already full.

"Lucy in a mood again today?" Luke adjusted the camouflage-colored cap on his head.

"When ain't she in a mood?" Another of the men lit a cigarette and laughed.

"She's just busy and tired." Katie filled the last cup. "Can I get you guys anything else?"

"Thanks, sweetie, but we're fine for now." Luke nodded toward the door. "Here comes old Joe."

Katie glanced at the clock on the wall. She could set her watch by Joe Norman. For the past five years, he pushed through the diner's door every morning at 6:45.

Carrying two breakfast specials, Lucy grumbled, "Here comes Mr. Moneybags."

Well-known around town, Joe Norman was not particularly popular. He didn't flaunt his money, but everyone knew he had plenty. In the town of Silver Springs, Missouri, where people were scraping to get by, Joe stood out like a teenager in a retirement home. He didn't dress fancy: jeans, a button-down shirt, and a cap like every other fellow. But clean-shaven, and no trace of grease under the fingernails, his appearance was a far cry from the other scruffy regulars.

"Do you want his table today?" Katie asked as Lucy shuffled past.

"Not today or any other day. The tip he leaves won't buy water." Lucy kept moving.

Katie winced. She appreciated a nice tip as much as anyone, but held to the philosophy, 'What a man does with his money is his business.'

Pot of coffee in one hand and menu in the other, Katie approached Joe's table. "Good morning, Joe. Coffee?"

"Sure thing, Sunshine. How are you today?"

Katie never ceased to be impressed by the sincerity in his voice. Many asked, but few really cared how she fared, as long as they got their coffee. "Doing good, Joe. Pretty busy, but that's a good thing."

"How's Lucy?"

"Lucy is Lucy. She's fine, I guess." With her cantankerous disposition, Lucy was hard to read. Katie was sure her mood would be the same if she had an abscessed tooth or if she won the lottery. She had never known such an ill-tempered person, but for some reason Joe always asked about her.

"I'll have biscuits and gravy this morning. As cold as it is, I need something that'll stick to my ribs."

Katie chuckled. Joe was skinny as a table leg. "Don't look to me like anything sticks to your ribs."

"Why's Lucy wearing a coat?" Joe frowned.

The ill-tempered waitress was pouring coffee at another table.

"Her heat went out last night and she's still chilled. She should warm up soon."

"What's wrong with her heat, if you don't mind my asking?"

Katie leaned down and whispered, "Out of gas and no money for more. But she'd kill me if she knew I said anything."

Joe nodded and Katie went about her daily routine. After eating breakfast and paying at the register, he left. She cleared his table and pocketed the tip. One thin dime.

"Did you get rich off the old man today?" An ugly laugh permeated Katie's ears.

With a forced smile, she turned to Lucy and acknowledged, "It might buy water."

The next morning Lucy arrived at work wearing an expression Katie had never seen on her face. It was by no means a smile. It was a look of confusion.

"What's wrong?" she asked as Lucy hung

her coat in the closet.

"I've got gas," Lucy blurted out.

Katie exploded in laughter. It was priceless. Thank heavens the coffee drinkers were not there yet.

"Not that kind of gas, you moron!" Lucy was livid. "Propane! Somebody filled my tank. Who on earth would do such a fool thing?"

Katie sobered quickly. "You mean you don't know where it came from?"

"I called the gas company and they said it was paid for anonymously. Who does that?"

Katie immediately thought of Joe. But it couldn't have been 'big-tipper' Joe. "I don't know. But with the temperature at zero, I'd be thankful I had a guardian angel, whoever it is."

"Yeah, well, I didn't ask for help." Lucy grabbed an apron and left the doors swinging and Katie dazed as she stomped into the kitchen.

Joe came through the front door at the usual 6:45 a.m. Katie thought he was walking slower and looked pale. "You okay, Joe?"

"Cold weather sure plays havoc with the arthritis. But I'm fine." The old man's smile could warm the coldest day. "Thanks for asking, Sunshine."

Fond of the affectionate nickname he'd

given her, she smiled, poured his coffee, took his order, and scurried to the kitchen. She was taking another order when Lucy let out a scream that would wake the dead – almost. It didn't wake Joe.

Luke Mason knocked over a chair in his rush to Joe's crumpled body. "Call 911," he shouted. "Now!"

When the paramedics pronounced Joe "dead at the scene," Luke snorted, "Didn't take special training to figure that out. You girls better hang out the 'Closed' sign and sit a while."

Most of the coffee crowd attended Joe Norman's graveside service. To Katie's surprise, Lucy was there. "Ain't no big deal," she shrugged. "Just thought it'd be respectful."

Two weeks later Katie still found herself looking at the clock at 6:45 each morning. She missed the old man and his smile. A shiver ran down her spine. With a towel, she wiped a tear and went back to work.

A gust of cold air blew through the open door and a distinguished-looking gentleman walked in. He removed his overcoat, displaying his tailor-made black suit and hung it on the seldom used coat rack near the door.

"I'll get this one." Lucy pushed past. "Coffee, sir?"

"I suppose. I also need to see Katie Billows and Lucy Golden. I was told I could find them here."

"I'm Lucy." Her eyes narrowed as she looked at the stranger. "Katie's over there."

"I need to talk with both of you when you can spare a few minutes."

"Might as well get it over with. Nobody here now but Luke, and he can take care of himself." Lucy had no time for salesmen or preachers, and he had to be one or the other. "Katie, this guy wants to talk to us. Bring the coffee pot."

Seated at the table, Katie and Lucy watched and waited as the stranger took a long sip of coffee.

"Ladies, my name is Brandon Book. I've been Joe Norman's attorney for many years."

"Hold it right there, mister." Lucy stood, red-faced and nostrils flared. "We had nothing to do with what happened to that old man. If you're here to sue somebody, you've come to the wrong place."

"I assure you, miss, I'm not here to sue anyone." The attorney shifted in his seat. "I'm here about Joe's will."

Curious and speechless, Lucy sat.

"Go ahead, Mr. Book. I think you've got

our full attention," Katie said.

At the next table Luke was all ears.

"Well, I have two letters. My instructions are to read them to you. The complete will is in my office, but these letters spell it out. Joe wrote them."

"Letters for us?" Katie asked in disbelief. The lump in her throat made the words barely audible.

The man opened an envelope. "Miss Billows, I'll read yours first. 'Katie, I was a terrible tipper. Many days I wanted to leave a hundred-dollar bill but couldn't. You have an infectious smile, and I never wanted to wonder if you were sincere or just trying to charm money out of an old fool. When you've got money, you tend to see ulterior motives behind everyone's actions. You can't put a price on 'Sunshine', but I'm leaving you one million dollars to match your million-dollar smile. I guess you can call it one last tip. Sincerely, Joe.'"

Katie gasped. Luke grinned, and Lucy turned beet red. "I'd have waited on the old fool for a million bucks," she hissed.

"I have another letter, Miss Golden. Please be patient."

Katie thought the lawyer had a peculiar look on his face and a note of disdain in his voice.

"Get on with it. Some people have to

work," Lucy snapped.

The lawyer opened the second envelope. He had a captivated audience. With sad eyes he apologized to the waitress. "I'm sorry, miss. I urged him to talk to you before he died, but he was hard headed." The lawyer read the second letter aloud. "'Lucy, I was overseas when my daughter gave birth to my only grandchild. Thinking they were too young for the responsibility, she and her husband placed the little girl with an adoption agency. A few weeks later, they were killed in a car crash. I searched for many years for my granddaughter. Finally a private detective led me here. That granddaughter was the only family I had left.

Lucy, the remainder of my estate is yours, as my granddaughter. Brandon can give you the exact amount, but it's around twenty million. I never told you who I was because I hoped you would learn to like me, not my money. Sadly, that never happened. But it has been a joy to spend my years near my granddaughter. There is enough money for many lifetimes, but it couldn't buy my happiness. Hopefully it will put a smile on your face. With love, Grandpa Joe.'"

Tears cascaded down Lucy's cheeks. "Why didn't he tell me? I've known for a long time I was adopted. They always made me feel like they'd done me a great favor, but I've seen dogs treated better."

Katie and Luke watched as the ill-tempered waitress tried to regain her composure. "All I've ever wanted was family. All this time and he never said a word. He has to be the most selfish person I've ever met."

Luke's weathered fist hit the table hard. "If this ain't a clear case of the skunk saying the polecat stinks! Missy, if you want selfish, take a look in the mirror. I'm surprised the man left you a dime."

Every eye was on the old coffee drinker. "But if it's family you want, I'm right here. Your daddy, my son, died in that car crash. Joe sensed his time was short. So a couple of weeks ago he told me who you were. I promised to keep quiet. I guess I was hoping, like Joe, that you had a heart. It's a shame he had to die before you let it show."

Months passed. If Lucy spent a dime of the inheritance, no one could tell. She came to work every day, but the alteration of her disposition was unmistakable.

"Morning, Katie." With a bounce in her step, Lucy carried the steaming pot to the table of regulars.

"Hey, Lucy, when you gonna splurge with some of that money?" The room filled with laughter. The customer pushed his point. "That was quite a bundle the old man left you."

Silence filled the room as Lucy filled Luke's cup slowly. "His name was Joe, and he gave me something more valuable than money." She stopped and pecked her new-found grandpa on the cheek. "He gave me family."

THE TWENTY-EGG CAKE

Now before everyone gets his or her cholesterol-conscious knickers in a knot, let me explain. The recipe only called for five eggs. Being the Betty Crocker that I am, I used twenty.

It all began after a trip to a local black walnut festival. I had picked up a pamphlet with some enticing recipes. Every holiday at my parents' home I took the same tired dish— baked beans. It seemed time to try something different and I knew everybody loved walnuts. What a surprise and delight I would give them with a three-layer black walnut cake. They would all be amazed at my culinary skill.

Being very good at following step-by-step instructions, this cake would be a breeze. Everything was going nicely. I really should bake from scratch more often. The third step instructed me to add the five egg yolks. So I separated the eggs, mixed in the yolks and threw away the whites.

Imagine my surprise when step seven instructed me to beat the egg whites. Perhaps I should have read the entire recipe before I started. But this was just a minor glitch. I had more eggs. After separating them, I put the whites in the bowl I had previously used to measure the sugar. If there is one chore I hate, it is washing dishes. So I had to economize my mess.

After beating the whites for at least ten minutes the only thing getting stiff was my arm from holding the portable mixer. After fifteen minutes I surrendered and phoned Mrs. Know-It-All. When she answered, I asked, "Mom, how long do you have to beat egg whites before they get stiff?"

Her reply, "Not long at all."

"But I have been beating them for fifteen minutes and nothing's happened," I wailed.

"Fifteen minutes? Good grief, what have you done wrong?"

Oh sure, blame me. It never occurred to her that the eggs could be hen-house rejects. "Well, I am beating them in the same bowl that I measured the sugar in, but what difference would that make?"

"That is your problem. The bowl has to be completely clean."

After mumbling thanks, I got off the phone. The egg whites were not forming a stiff peak, but the same could not be said for my blood pressure. I was out of eggs. Luckily, at least on this day, my mother-in-law is our next-door neighbor. So I phoned her and she agreed to give me a half dozen eggs.

A quick trip to my mother-in-law's, and I was ready to get cooking. This cake was not going to get the better of me. After separating another five eggs, I put the whites in a totally clean bowl. I started to walk to the table where the mixer was patiently waiting. Oops! My apron got caught on a cabinet drawer knob and yanked me backward, but the eggs kept going forward, sloshing out of the bowl and onto the floor. I had never dropped an egg before. What a day to start. The egg casualty count was now fifteen.

There was absolutely no way I was calling my mother-in-law for more eggs. I would rather streak through the local mall than admit I had dropped five eggs on the floor. I cleaned up the mess, took off the apron, and drove three miles to the grocery store. I purchased two-dozen eggs. Surely that would be enough to cover any further disasters.

I returned home, separated five more eggs, and finished that cake. My family loved my twenty-egg cake and the story of its creation. Glutton for punishment that I am, I have made the cake several times since. It was a lot of trouble, but it melts in your mouth. Strange as it might seem, I have never needed more than five eggs since that first eventful cake.

Cakes in a box were made for people like me. Add water, mix and bake. No muss, no fuss, and the chickens can rest easier.

LOST AND FOUND

Chicken sizzled in the electric skillet. Beans simmered on the stove. Lois opened the oven door and pulled out a pan of golden cornbread. Every Wednesday evening she cooked supper for her only son, Gavin. It was probably the only home-cooked meal he got all week. Heaven knows that wife of his would need a map to find her way around a kitchen.

"Mom, we're here."

The sound of Gavin's voice brought a smile to her face. Tolerating his wife was a small price to pay for time with her son. "I'm in the kitchen."

"Something sure smells good." Gavin

gave her a quick peck on the cheek. "Fried chicken? You're gonna spoil me."

"You're already spoiled," Alex said. The words were colder than water in a frozen pond.

Lois faced her daughter-in-law. "I suppose he is, Alex, but who else have I got to fuss over?" She hoped her words sounded lighter than her heart felt. Since her husband died three years ago, Gavin was all the family she had. "Grandchildren would have been nice," Lois muttered.

"Mother!"

"I'm sorry." She had better start digging her way out of this hole. "It's time to eat." Maybe with food in her mouth there wouldn't be room for her foot. Gavin made it clear years ago that Alex wanted a career, not children, and talk of grandchildren, or the lack thereof, would not be tolerated.

In their small town in the Ozarks, nobody's business was private. Lois heard the muffled remarks when she walked down the street. People felt sorry for the widow with no grandchildren. She fought the urge to feel sorry for herself, but once in a while she lost the battle.

As Gavin and Alex took their usual seats, Lois placed a platter of chicken on the table.

"It looks great, Mom," Gavin said as she shifted in her chair. Thank heavens for a son who didn't hold a grudge.

"How are things at work?"

She listened as her son prattled on about his week, and she watched Alex push food around her plate. Wouldn't want that toothpick to gain an ounce.

"So, Mom, what've you been up to?"

Lois smiled, pushed away from the table and walked to the cabinet. She opened a drawer and retrieved a box. Setting the black box on the table, she opened the lid. "What do you think?"

All eating stopped. "Mother, where on earth did you get that thing?"

"I bought it at the gun shop downtown." She turned toward her daughter-in-law. "Don't you think it's pretty, Alex? I love the pearl handle."

"Oh, for Pete's sake, Lois. Nobody buys a firearm because it's pretty. People are killed every day with their own guns. What were you thinking? Do you even know how to use it?"

She knew better than to expect support from Alex. If a snootier woman walked the face of the earth, Lois didn't want to meet her. She would love to apply duct tape to the flapper beneath Alex's nose.

A thorn in her side from day one, Lois never understood what her son saw in his wife. Even with his wife's career, Gavin worked double shifts whenever possible to keep designer labels hanging in the closet. Only the best for Alex. Lois smiled. Gavin was the best.

"Mother, why are you smiling? This is no laughing matter. Alex asked if you know how to use the gun." Irritation filled Gavin's words.

"Of course I know how to use it. The man at the store showed me." Tired of being scolded like a child, Lois placed the box in a kitchen drawer and poured herself a cup of coffee.

"There is no way he gave you proper instruction at the store," Gavin insisted.

"Lois, what possessed you to buy such a thing?" Alex glared with righteous indignation at the closed drawer holding the object of contention.

"You know there's been a rash of burglaries in the neighborhood. I don't like feeling helpless."

"You have no business with a gun," her son said.

"You're entitled to your perspective, but it makes me feel safe."

Lois served cake and re-filled the coffee cups. They endured strained conversation for the remainder of the visit, and sadly, she was grateful when her son made a lame excuse to leave early.

With the two nervous Nellies gone, she locked the door and headed upstairs. Regret raced through her mind. What had she expected? Gavin hated guns and she knew it. His father tried years ago to interest him in hunting to no avail. It was a bond they couldn't share.

She crawled into bed and stared into the darkness, tired. Tired of the daily grind. Tired of being alone, and sick and tired of her self-righteous daughter-in-law.

Two days passed. Gavin had phoned to thank her for supper, but no mention of the gun was made. Maybe he wouldn't make a boulder out of a pebble.

Lois opened the kitchen drawer, picked up the gun case, and began to perspire. It was light, too light. She unlatched the lid and gasped at the sight of the empty container. The plush red felt held only an imprint where the gun used to be. It was there a couple of days ago, wasn't it? She shuddered as her son's words echoed in her mind. "You have no business with a gun."

How was she going to tell them? She had owned a gun for a few short days and it was lost. She had to find it. Words flew from her mouth that would make a minister blush as Lois threw objects out of the drawer. It wasn't there. Without stopping to replace anything, she yanked open the next drawer and unloaded it onto the table. How the devil does a gun disappear?

Was this the onset of some mental deterioration? Why hadn't she tried to make coffee in the blender or paraded to the mailbox in her birthday suit? Instead, her first act of lunacy was to lose a gun. Her face turned scarlet as her mind raced from one manic thought to another.

Lois threw open the pantry door, giving the hinges a work-out. A jacket fell from a hook onto the floor. Finding two dollars in the pocket did not bring joy. She rummaged through the shelves. No gun in the pantry.

She tossed the kitchen with the expertise of a first-rate burglar. A jar of jalapeño peppers hit the floor and shattered. How she wished this was her biggest mess.

Defeated, she plopped into a chair. The thought of telling Gavin was bad enough, but the idea of sitting through a lecture from that wife of his was intolerable.

Sitting accomplished nothing. The gun had to be in the house somewhere. Racking her brain, she tried to remember where she might have put it. The last time she saw the blasted thing, it was in the case. She had placed the case in the cabinet drawer; at least she thought she did. Her head throbbed.

Helen! Yes, she'd call Helen. She picked up the phone and dialed the number of her best friend and next-door neighbor. "Helen, I need help."

The conversation was short, but Lois relied on her friend. True to form, Helen knocked on the door within five minutes.

"Are you all right, Lois?"

"Not really."

Her friend stepped into the kitchen wearing a puzzled frown. "If this is your idea of spring cleaning, you need a refresher course. What's going on?"

Lois sighed. "I've lost something important and you have to help me find it."

"It must be awfully important to cause such a fuss, not to mention one heck of a mess." Helen shook her head. "Of course I'll help you. Now, what are we looking for?"

Lois stared at the floor and mumbled, "A gun."

"Thunderation, Lois, did you say gun?"

"Yes, Helen." Desperation filled her voice. "I just bought it a few days ago, and I swear the last time I saw the blasted thing it was in that case." She pointed to the empty container on the table. "I put it in the cabinet drawer and today it's gone. I've combed the kitchen from top to bottom. It's not here. What am I going to do?"

Helen's hand on her shoulder provided

strength and comfort she hadn't expected. "Lois, we're not getting any younger. I'm always putting something in one place, only to discover it somewhere else. Why, just the other day I found the paper towels in the refrigerator. I would have sworn I put them in the pantry. We'll search this house till we find that gun."

Lois nodded.

"Since you've already taken care of the kitchen, let's try your bedroom. Maybe you put it in a drawer there."

"But I don't remember..."

"Precisely. You don't remember, so we will search the entire house."

"I feel like such a dimwit," Lois said as she emptied the contents of her underwear drawer onto the bed. "One thing's for sure, I'm getting rid of that thing as soon as we find it. The stress of having a gun in the house is gonna kill me before a burglar gets the chance."

"I remember this." Helen came out of the closet holding a pink sweater. "I always liked this sweater. You never wear it anymore."

"We're not here to take inventory," Lois snapped.

"I think what we need to take is a break," Helen suggested. "You've probably been at this all morning. Did you even eat breakfast?"

"Not even coffee."

"And it's time for lunch. Let's go eat a sandwich and re-group."

Seated at the kitchen table, Lois had to admit her stomach was beginning to protest being ignored. Pushing things to one side of the table, the two friends each made a sandwich.

Lois glanced at the kitchen clock. It would soon be time for the weather forecast. "Shall we watch the news?" The idiotic banter of the noon newscasters, while waiting for the local meteorologist, might take her mind off her problem for a little while.

"Why not?"

Lois turned on the small television on the cabinet and couldn't believe her eyes. Yellow crime scene tape surrounded Gavin's house. She gasped.

"Police are investigating a potential homicide that took place this morning. One person is being questioned in connection with the incident. This is the first homicide in this quiet Ozarks town in over ten years. Details are being withheld pending notification of family. We will have more on this story as it unfolds."

In shock, Lois grabbed her purse and ran to the garage. That despicable woman had killed her son. Although they refused to give names, she knew Gavin's home when she saw it, and according to the news, it was now the scene of a crime.

Helen snatched the keys from her hand. "I'll drive."

Lois nodded. In an angry haze, she rode to the police station in silence. Why hadn't they called her? Her only son was dead and she had to hear it on the news. Tears streamed down her face. Where would she find the strength to bury her only son?

As Helen pulled into a parking space, Lois wiped her eyes. First things first. That hateful woman would not get away with killing her son.

Taking a deep breath, Lois marched up the steps and into the station with Helen close behind. She was about to demand answers when Gavin walked around the corner in handcuffs, escorted by two officers. He looked at her and hung his head.

The next sight caused Lois to faint dead away. One of the officers was carrying her pretty, pearl-handled gun.

HOT AND BOTHERED

"Men work shirtless every day. Why shouldn't I?" She winked at the cat perched on the window ledge, unbuttoned her blouse, and threw it across the room. Next went the jeans, but Maude drew a line at underwear. A lady has to keep her dignity.

"This bra is what's really hot." She laughed and sent the uncomfortable undergarment sailing through the air over her shoulder.

Maude heard the faint voice of a man whisper, "She's crazy."

She turned to see a stranger, standing in the archway between her kitchen and living room, wide-eyed and wearing her bra on his head.

A thief – a murderer – or worse, a rapist? Good heavens. She looked down at her nearly nude self. I've done half the job for him. Wait. Did he say crazy? People are scared of folks who are nuts. Watching Lethal Weapon might finally pay off, but did she have Mel's acting ability? Her mind raced. I can't say I'm crazy, can I? Don't insane people think they're fine?

"I'm not crazy. You're late," she blurted as she snatched the bra from his head.

"Late?" The man looked bewildered.

Humiliation surged through her body. Her mind shifted into overdrive. "Yes, late. You were supposed to be here three hours ago to mow the yard. It won't mow itself, you know." Without waiting for a response, she pointed out the kitchen window. "The mower is in the shed."

She couldn't believe her luck when the man turned and left. With a weak smile, Maude realized her lethal weapon against the intruder was her sixty-year-old body, and for today, she was grateful. He was gone.

She pulled her jeans up over trembling knees and fastened her bra. Maude couldn't dress fast enough. Her nervous fingers fumbled with blouse buttons. A familiar motor roared to life in the backyard. It couldn't be.

Out the kitchen window, she stared in amazement as the stranger made circles around the yard with the old push-mower. She should call the police. Phone in hand, she shook her head and returned it to the holder. What would she tell them? That she had been washing dishes in the buff and a burglar was mowing her yard? She'd be the laughingstock of the county.

Too scared and naked earlier, she now took full inventory of the man. Tall and thin, he was in his early twenties, but to Maude that was a boy. His gaunt face revealed hunger, not a hardened criminal. It was too hot to be mowing in the middle of the day. For a moment her heart softened.

Blast it all. He saw her naked. What gave him the right to walk in without knocking? The boy took long strides and kept mowing.

Why today? Why had the air conditioner quit when she was in the middle of canning tomatoes? If she had followed her instinct and bought a new fan when Wal-Mart had them on sale, she wouldn't be in this fix. With the only fan on the farm missing its electrical cord, she chose today to be totally reckless and strip in the kitchen.

Maude lived alone on a secluded farm

with the nearest neighbors several miles away. A long, private lane led from the main road to her house. Nobody ever bothered her — until today. Who was the man in the yard?

Anger replaced embarrassment. If she wanted to strip down and paint herself purple, it was nobody's business. She was at home. He was the intruder.

Maude returned to the sink and glanced often out the window while she washed the dishes. Hot as green beans in a pressure cooker, she wiped her forehead and face with the dishtowel. Perspiring was for snooty town ladies. She sweated.

The mowing finished, the man knocked on the kitchen door. She opened it and invited him in.

On the table sat a plate of sandwiches, a pitcher of lemonade, and two glasses. Being polite couldn't hurt, and Maude hoped to learn more about her peculiar intruder. "I'm going to have a snack. Would you care to join me?" She took a seat and tried unsuccessfully to erase their first encounter from her mind.

The young man gobbled down the sandwiches. Maude knew she'd made the right assessment. This boy was no threat. She placed a twenty-dollar bill on the table.

"The yard looks nice. But if I were you,

I'd get here earlier tomorrow to do the trimming."

A puzzled look on his face, the young man took the money, nodded, and left. That was that. She locked the door behind him.

Much to her surprise, the stranger returned early the next morning ready and willing to work. Her yard had never been trimmed so well. With all her other chores, she couldn't give it the attention it deserved. When he finished, Maude again invited him in, fed and paid him.

"My name is Jeff Turner," the young man said shyly as he pocketed his pay.

"Well, Jeff, I'd be happy if you'd come back next week and mow my yard again. You can even use the mower with the seat on it."

"You have a riding mower?" The boy was dumbfounded. "I didn't see it."

"It's not in the shed. I keep it in the barn," Maude replied with a twinkle in her eyes. "By the way, have you made a determination about my mental condition?"

Jeff shook his head. "Yes, ma'am. You're crazy. Crazy like a fox."

"A fox that had a lapse in judgment, I'm afraid. I don't normally –"

"Ma'am, there's no easy way to go about this, so I'll put my cards on the table.

Yesterday, when I arrived at your front door, I thought you called for me to come in."

Maude's face was hot. That's what she got for talking to the cat.

The young man continued. "I am very sorry I intruded on your privacy. Truth is, I'm the new minister and I just came to introduce myself." He placed all her money on the table. "I should have said something yesterday, but to be honest, the seminary didn't prepare me for an encounter of that sort."

"But you came back," she stammered. "And you were so hungry."

"Yes, ma'am. Push-mowing a yard tends to work up an appetite."

Maude's face flushed.

"If my yard work is done, I'd better go visit more folks."

Speechless, she nodded and shook the outstretched hand.

He smiled and said, "I hope we'll be seeing more of each other."

Maude blushed. Hadn't he seen more than enough?

LIMITS

Hal stopped the monotonous counting of ceiling tiles. There would be time for that later. Plenty of time.

His mind wandered to his childhood, and a smile crossed his face. Mama was none too happy when he came home from school sporting a black eye and told him fighting would not be tolerated. She said every young man needed to get a grip on their temper.

Though it happened sixty years ago, his mother's words were imbedded in his memory. "Son, when you get upset or mad, just close your eyes and picture my face."

He couldn't understand how, or why, her method worked, but it did.

When Beth walked out and left him after five years of marriage, he closed his eyes and saw Mama's face. When their three-year-old son, Danny, cried for his mother, Hal comforted him the best he could. Many nights after he tucked Danny in bed, Hal sat in silence with closed eyes.

Raising his son alone was a struggle. It gave him a profound appreciation for his own mother, who raised him by herself after his father was killed in a train accident. Mama died when he was twenty, but she packed a lot of teaching into those years. He'd often wondered if she sensed her time was limited. Then again, he remembered her famous words. "I'm not raising a spoiled brat. I'm raising a young man who won't be ashamed to face himself in the mirror."

Mama's teachings stuck. Hal passed the lessons on to his son and prayed for the best. Although he had doubts about his weather-beaten face being a comfort to anyone, Hal relayed his boyhood story to Danny and encouraged him to "close your eyes and picture my face whenever you get mad."

Mama's trick worked again. Danny never had a fight, but Hal had seen him standing red-faced with clenched fists and closed eyes. Hal would close his eyes and gather strength to guide his son.

Now in his forties and married to his college sweetheart, Danny had two children, and from everything Hal had seen, his grandkids were raised right.

With a loud clang, he was jolted back to the present and his current surroundings.

"Dad, what on earth are you doing here?"

Hal smiled at his son. "Well, I got myself arrested."

"I can see that, but why?"

"I shot the television," Hal answered very matter-of-factly.

"You can't shoot the TV." Danny paced in front of the cell door.

"Why not? It's my TV."

"Okay, it's your television. You can shoot it if you want."

"Then why did they arrest me?" Hal scratched his head.

"Sheriff Gates said it's illegal to discharge a firearm within the city limits."

"But that's where the television is. You mean I have to haul it out of town to shoot it?"

"No, Dad," Danny said, exasperated.

Hal watched his son close his eyes, only to snap them open again.

"The trick not working?" He regretted

the words but couldn't retrieve them.

"It's hard for your face to have a calming effect when it's behind bars," Danny said.

Hal nodded, but remained silent.

"Dad?"

"What, son?"

"Why did you shoot the television?"

"I got mad," Hal answered.

"But didn't you close your eyes? What about grandma's face?"

"Grandma never had to put up with cable."

THE CLEAR BLUE SKY

Laundry hung motionless on the decrepit old clothesline. Ruth preferred to see it flapping in the wind. A breeze gave the towels a fresh scent and made the hundred-degree heat almost tolerable. Almost. Relief was nowhere in sight on this August day in 1928.

Freshly canned jars of green beans lined the shelf in the tool shed. Ruth's husband, Ben, claimed he didn't have time to fix the clothesline, but made time to put a cook stove in the shed. The homestead of Ben's parents, the outbuilding had a suitable chimney. Planting a late crop of beans so they'd have enough to get through the winter was a good idea, but after she overheated the house while canning the first crop, Ben wasted no time fixing a place for her to can in the building out back. The beans would taste good in December, but sleeping outside in July had only been fun for Holly, their ten-year-old daughter.

A tranquil smile crossed Ruth's face. She wiped beads of sweat from her forehead and watched Holly and her best friend, Mary, pull a rusty red wagon down the dirt road. Determined to make ice cream, the girls were more than eager to make the trip to the little country store for a block of ice. Giggles and laughter accompanied the squeak of the wagon coming down the road.

With head tilted back and eyes closed, Ruth took a deep breath and exhaled. Children had no concept of hot and cold. Those two little girls would jump rope and play in the yard until their faces were as red as vine-ripened tomatoes. Many times Ruth had interrupted their fun to offer them water, lemonade, or iced tea.

Holly and Mary were equally oblivious in cold weather. Their cheeks red and hands chafed, the girls would play in snow until Ruth ordered them in. She sighed. No chance of snow today. The coldest thing she could hope to enjoy was a nice bowl of homemade ice cream.

The girls pulled their purchase, one block of ice in a burlap sack, through the front gate. "Mom, we got it," Holly yelled.

Ruth hurried to mix the ingredients. Hot and cold might not bother the girls, but waiting was a different story. Ten-year-olds have lots of time but little patience.

With the mixture in its container, Ruth carried it to the porch. "Get the maul so I can bust the ice."

Two barefooted girls scampered to the tool shed. Shoes on children were unheard of in summertime. Their little feet began to callous at the first hint of spring. Like the clothesline, the shed was in need of repair, but would have to wait until Ben harvested the fall crops. Ruth worried about him working alone in this heat, but there was no money to hire help. Ice cream would hit the spot when he came in from the field.

While she got the rock salt from the back porch, Holly and Mary returned with the maul. Not stout enough to carry the tool, a trail accompanied the little footprints through the powdery dirt and brittle August grass as they dragged it.

"How's your dad today, Mary?" When his wife died eight years ago, John Banks was left with the sad task of raising Mary alone. Bad luck followed him like odor trails a skunk. A carpenter by trade, he'd fallen from a roof. His injuries left him in a wheelchair.

"He's doing okay. He gets around in that contraption and does quite a bit. He's fixing a chair today for old lady-- I mean Mrs. Anderson."

Ruth smiled at the girl's misstep. Everyone referred to Maude Anderson as Old Lady Anderson, not because of her age, but because she was the community busybody. "I'm glad to hear he has work."

"Daddy said he's surprised at all the odd jobs he can do sitting down."

"Are we going to make ice cream or not?" Holly interrupted.

"We're going to make ice cream," Ruth assured her impatient daughter.

Maul in hand, she set the burlap sack on the ground. After a few hard whacks, there was enough ice chipped off the block to get started. "Girls, I have to get my kitchen mess cleaned up. Holler when you need more ice, and remember, you have to keep cranking." Ruth opened the screen door and stepped inside. Outdoors or in made no difference today. The air so thick you could slice it like pie, she hoped Ben would finish in the field soon.

From the kitchen, Ruth listened as the girls cranked and chuckled. She dried and placed the last jelly jar glass in the cabinet.

From the porch Holly called out, "Momma, we need more ice."

"Be right there." Ruth stepped outside and gasped. The beautiful, clear blue had been replaced by an ominous green tint in the dark southwestern sky. Green was a sign of hail, but something deep in her gut told Ruth this was worse.

Trees swayed as the wind picked up speed. "Mary, you'd better get home. Looks like we're in for a storm."

"Yes, ma'am, I have to take care of Daddy." The girl took off in a run for the little white house an eighth of a mile away.

"But, Momma, what about our ice cream?"

"Not today, Holly." Ruth headed for the line to rescue the clothes whipping in the wind.

"Forget those clothes," Ben yelled as he ran toward them. "Get to the cellar. This is a bad one." Without hesitation his strong arms scooped up Holly and his legs picked up speed as he headed for the backyard storm cellar.

With Ruth on his heels, hail pelted them as Ben set Holly on the ground long enough to open the cellar door. They scrambled down the steps into the dark, damp haven. The cellar housed their yearly crop of potatoes and onions, as well as a host of spiders and bugs. Today the insects didn't merit a second thought. Something much bigger, and more deadly, was outside the door.

"Daddy, what's that noise? Trains don't go by here."

Grateful for the dark, Ruth knew her face would betray the fear that seized her body. She stopped groping for the candle and matches on the shelf and shuddered as she listened to the storm rage.

"Honey, I'm pretty sure it's a tornado. But we're safe in here." Ben was calm and reassuring.

"Daddy, what about Mary?" Fear permeated the little girl's voice.

Ruth's stomach churned and a lump formed in her throat. The Banks had no cellar. Even if they did, Mary was too small to carry her father into it.

As quickly as it came, the monster was gone. Ben opened the door and they climbed the stairs to survey the damage.

Repair was no longer a possibility since most of the decrepit old clothesline was tangled in an uprooted tree in the field. Once clean laundry hung muddy and twisted among broken branches. The tool shed was also a casualty. Ruth moaned. All her canned goods were gone. All her hard work blown to smithereens.

"It missed the house." Ben shook his head. "The barn wasn't so lucky."

"Momma, look." Holly pointed toward Mary's house. At that moment Ruth knew she could never live long enough to forget the horror on Holly's face.

Fear gripped Ruth's heart. Most of the Banks' house was gone.

The graveside service was short. The minister read the usual comforting words, and the man in the wheelchair rocked back and forth quietly sobbing and repeating the same words. "Why? Why?"

"They say the little girl had just got home and managed to push John into the archway between the kitchen and living room." Maude Anderson was full of details for anyone who'd listen. "When the twister took the roof, she was hit in the head with a ceiling beam. Heaven only knows what happened to my chair."

Ruth turned her back on the heartless woman, and through a mist of tears, looked down at her own precious daughter. Holly's cheeks were wet with sorrow. She lifted her head. Their eyes met.

"Momma, why did you have to send Mary home?" The voice that giggled three days ago now sounded accusatory. The eyes that sparkled with mischievousness were dull in mourning. A clear blue sky rapidly turned dark and produced a monster that took her friend and forever shattered her childhood innocence.

Ruth had no satisfactory answers. As tears streamed down her face, she whispered, "I don't know, honey. I don't know."

BIG EARS AND BAND AIDS

The smell of hot pizza wafted from the take-out box. Julie pulled the car into the garage. Bryan didn't like fast food but he wouldn't cook.

Pizza in hand, she limped into the kitchen. Her feet ached after a bad choice of shoes. But she had to look stylish. Why did she still feel the need to impress her mother?

"I'm home," she called out and placed the pizza on the table. "Is Corey next door?" She already knew the answer. Her husband was too busy for their five-year-old son. Busy taking a nap.

"You made it home." He opened the box.

"I'm starved. I guess this will do."

"What about Corey?"

"He's at Debbie's. I figured he'd rather play over there."

"I'll be right back." He had worked all day, but the least he could have done was pick up their son. She hadn't had an easy day herself.

She thanked Debbie and headed Corey toward home. If they didn't hurry the pizza would be cold or gone. She wasn't hungry, but little boys need to eat.

Seated at the table, Bryan and Corey wasted no time grabbing a slice of pizza.

"So, how did your mom's liposuction go?" Bryan took another bite.

Before Julie could answer, Corey asked, "What is suction?"

How many times had she warned her husband that children have big ears? Her mind struggled for an explanation.

Bryan blurted, "Vacuum cleaners have suction."

"Did grandma get a new cleaner?"

"No, Corey." Red-faced and angry, Julie took charge of the conversation. "Grandma had surgery called liposuction."

"They used a vacuum cleaner on grandma?" The boy's eyes were wide.

Bryan chuckled and picked up another slice of pizza.

"I suppose they did in a way. Grandma had some stuff that needed to be gotten rid of." Her little boy didn't need to know his grandmother was so vain she couldn't stand the thought of a few extra pounds. She abhorred the idea of exercise but had no qualms about surgery.

Julie winced. It couldn't be heartburn. She hadn't touched the pizza. Exhausted from spending the day at the hospital with her mother, she hoped for a peaceful evening at home. Had her husband and mother given her an ulcer?

With morning sunlight beaming through the kitchen window, Julie Bennett scrambled eggs in one skillet while bacon sizzled in another.

Bryan parked his posterior in a chair and sipped coffee from a mug that proclaimed WORLD'S BEST DAD. Corey insisted on the mug as a Father's Day gift.

Julie wiped a tear and put breakfast on the table. Tousling her son's hair, her heart yearned for there to be some truth in the words on the mug.

Bryan asked, "Are you going to your mom's today?"

"Corey and I are going to check on her this morning. I hope she was able to sleep last night."

"Aren't you going to eat?"

"I'm still having stomach problems." Aware of the worry on her five-year-old's face, she added, "Maybe I'll get something later."

"Don't you think it's time to see a doctor? This has gone on long enough."

Touched by her husband's concern, Julie answered, "I have an appointment this afternoon. But I'm sure it's nothing. I think it's just a nervous stomach."

"Probably, but it's time to be sure." He kissed her cheek. "Call if you need me. See you tonight."

"Bye, Daddy," Corey called after him.

The only acknowledgement the boy received was a raised hand and half-hearted wave as his father left for work.

Julie swallowed hard. She wanted so much more for her son. Corey was fine with the status quo, but he didn't know anything different. What was going to happen when he started school? How would he react when he saw fathers who were interested and spent time with their sons?

"Corey, wash you face. It's time to go visit grandma."

"Can I take her something?"

"Sure, honey. Did you draw a picture for her?"

"No. I want to take grandma my Band-Aids."

"Band-Aids?" Glad her husband had left for work, Julie imagined the belly laugh he would get from Corey's gift to grandma.

She glanced at the clock. "You'd better hurry. Wash your face and get the Band-Aids. We've got to go."

Julie retrieved her purse from the closet, pulled out the car keys, then sat in a chair and waited for Corey.

Her thoughts traveled back to her wedding day. They were so happy, with so many plans for the future. Those plans did not include a baby.

In all the excitement and thrill of love and romance, Julie and Bryan never discussed children. When she became pregnant a few months after the wedding, he didn't hide his displeasure.

"You know my dad ran out when I was a kid. I don't know anything about how to be a father," he said. "But if you want to have the baby, I understand. Just don't count on me to be super dad."

With all the naïveté of a woman in love, Julie expected Bryan to turn to mush at the sight of their newborn son. It didn't happen.

Never cruel to Corey, he remained aloof and disengaged as a father.

"Mom, I got 'em."

Her son's voice interrupted her thoughts.

Kneeling beside him, she looked at the bright box of Spiderman Band-Aids. "Grandma will love these."

In true grandma fashion, Julie's mother gushed over the "beautiful Band-Aids." Much to her grandson's delight, she insisted on wearing three of them right away.

Julie smiled and watched as Corey applied the colorful gifts to his grandma's arms. She gave thanks that her mother, with all her pride in appearance, understood the importance of a little boy's gift and the fragility of a young heart.

After dropping Corey off with her neighbor, Julie headed for the dreaded doctor's appointment.

She circled the crowded lot searching for a vacant parking space. Finally Julie pulled into a spot and took a deep breath. It would be nice to be parking at a restaurant and actually feel like eating.

She cranked up her courage and stepped out of the car. The doctor would get to the root of her problem, give her a prescription, and that would be that. She hoped.

Two weeks and several tests later, Julie and Bryan sat at the kitchen table.

"I've talked to Debbie. Corey is going to stay with her for a few days," Julie said.

"Okay."

"I think he needs to know what's going on."

"That's up to you."

She called for their son to turn off the television and come in the kitchen.

"Is it time to eat?" Corey looked puzzled by the empty table.

"No, honey," Julie said. "Sit down. I need to talk to you."

"Did I do something wrong?"

Why couldn't Bryan help her? She couldn't think about that now. "Son, you didn't do anything. I just want to tell you that I'm going to have surgery tomorrow. It's no big deal and I don't want you to worry. I have a bad gallbladder and the doctor is going to take it out. Then I'll feel much better."

With wide eyes, Corey asked, "Are you having suction like grandma?"

Realizing her son had seen how quickly his grandma recovered, Julie decided it best to not try to explain the different surgeries. After all, the doctor would be getting rid of something.

"I suppose I am having suction like grandma."

The five-year-old began sobbing uncontrollably.

"Corey, what's wrong? I'm going to be fine."

Through sobs and sniffles, he wailed, "I gave all my Band-Aids to grandma."

Bryan pushed his chair away from the table and stood.

Julie's heart ached. She needed his help and he couldn't miss Monday Night Football.

Her eyes widened as she watched the arms of the man she loved scoop Corey out of his chair. She held her breath.

"We'll be back soon," Bryan smiled. "I'm taking my son to buy Band-Aids."

She exhaled and smiled through a cascade of tears. Who needs Spiderman? Her superhero had finally emerged.

SPLASHDOWN

The screen door slapped shut as Janet walked out of the house and left a sink of dirty dishes, and furniture so dusty the grandkids could have a heyday writing their names with their fingers. The sunshine and pond bank called her name. Even in her fifties, she loved to fish. The mundane chores could wait. Summer was passing and she intended to drink in one more day in the sun.

A tackle box in one hand and fishing pole in the other, Janet strolled to the small pond on their forty-acre farm. She set the box on the bank and looked into the water. She watched a blue domed object, the size of her kitchen table, sink in the middle of the pond. What kind of trash had the neighbors discarded this time?

The Clarks moved in over a year ago, and Janet had been blessed with their trash on her property ever since. They would not spoil this day. The object, now underwater, was best forgotten. As she tied an artificial lure on her line a gurgling sound caught her attention.

Janet watched as the blue object rose to the surface and began to circle the pond. This was not the neighbor's trash. A faint hum emitted from the strange metallic orb as it passed a few feet in front of her and stopped near the bank.

Wide-eyed, she watched a door open, a ramp slide out, and two little beings scamper across to the bank. She dropped her pole. She had seen Leprechauns on television and in books but never in person.

"I told you to turn right at the city of steel and glass mountains. You never listen."

"Father says that is called New York City. It is no place to land. And how could I not listen? You talk all the time, just like your mother."

"What did you say about my mother?"

"Nothing, dear."

Janet shook her head. This could not be happening. Leprechaun aliens?

"Zini, look!" One of the miniature beings pointed a short finger at Janet.

She stood frozen. This was not the day of fishing she had in mind. These creatures looked like Leprechauns, but they had emerged from what she assumed was a spacecraft.

"Do you think it talks?" The alien still pointed.

"How would I know? I have never been here."

"I thought maybe your father might have told you."

Even in her stupor, Janet recognized sarcasm. She swallowed hard. "Hello." Her voice inaudible, she cleared her throat and tried again. "Hello. My name is Janet. Welcome to Missouri."

"Missouri?" The feminine alien turned and in a shrill voice shouted at her partner, "You said we were on Earth. When will you learn to ask for directions?"

"This is Earth," Janet explained. "Missouri is just a small part of it."

"I told you I knew where I was going." The little bearded alien put his hands on his hips. "When will you learn to trust my driving, Frill?"

"Maybe when you learn how to drive, Zini."

A nervous giggle escaped Janet's lips as

she watched the comical couple.

"Frill, we are being rude." The alien man with pointed ears scolded his companion. "Hello," he said to Janet in a pleasant, but squeaky voice. "My name is Zini and this is my wife, Frill. I suppose you are a bloblet."

"A bloblet? I don't know what you're talking about."

With a quizzical look on his face, the one called Zini asked, "Are you from Earth?"

"Yes," she replied.

"Just as I thought, you are a bloblet."

"Why are you calling me that? What is a bloblet?"

"That is what we call Earth beings like you. Why do you call us aliens and extraterrestrials?"

Stumped by the strange question, she decided to turn the tables. "I thought you said you've never been here. If this is your first visit, how do you know what we call you?"

Zini and Frill laughed. Zini replied, "We have television. Thanks to all your satellites, we see and hear quite a lot. Are you a Desperate Housewife?"

Janet laughed at the peculiar notion. "No, I'm a plain housewife. Most women are very different than we are portrayed on television."

"We understand." Frill smiled. "We are

not accurately depicted either."

Janet looked at the two small strangers. Never had she seen an alien with pointy ears and a white beard wearing an emerald green frock coat on television. In a full green and yellow polka dot skirt and matching yellow blouse, Frill looked ready for a square dance.

"May I ask why your spacecraft is in the pond? Did you crash? I thought you landed in fields."

"That is more television nonsense. I suppose you believe we create crop circles, too?" Zini narrowed his brown eyes at Janet.

"I don't know," she stammered, embarrassed to admit that until now she believed aliens to be a Hollywood hoax.

"Stop scaring the bloblet," Frill scolded. "Be polite."

"I am sorry. We are the visitors." Zini looked at Janet. "Father said we must always land in a body of water to cool our vehicle after entering the atmosphere. That is why we submerged temporarily. I believe bloblets call it a splashdown."

"What planet is your home?" These adorable aliens posed no obvious threat, so Janet decided to ask a few questions.

"We are not allowed to disclose that information. It is the one stipulation of our travel."

"I understand," she replied, although she didn't. "Why is your craft blue? I thought they were silver."

"I love blue," Frill gushed. "It was the only blue one at the dealership. Zini wanted a bright red, but I convinced him the blue would blend in with the sky. Silver is so last century."

"Was it expensive?" What was she thinking? She was not going to need a spaceship any time soon.

"Expensive?" Zini looked puzzled.

"That was a rude question. I'm sorry. Expensive means it cost a lot of money. You don't have to answer."

"We do not mind," Zini said. "We have no system like bloblets. We do not pay. Everyone gets what they need; no more, no less."

No monetary system. Janet was dumbfounded. Aliens, at least on television, were light years ahead in technology and intelligence. Perhaps that explained their presence. "Are you here looking for intelligent life form?"

Frill laughed uncontrollably, but Zini solemnly answered Janet's question. "We have read in our history books of our ancestors making many unsuccessful trips to your planet in search of higher intelligence. But that ended well over one hundred years ago."

Her mind whirled. How could the aliens have overlooked all the great thinkers and inventors? "Why did they stop looking?"

"Do you not watch television?" Zini appeared surprised. "Bloblets are destroying one another and their planet. I do not wish to insult, but how intelligent can you be?"

Janet looked at the visitors. Zini and Frill might be three feet tall, but she felt small in their presence. "I guess we do need to make a few changes."

"A few?"

She veered the conversation to another topic. "Why are you visiting Earth?" If it is such a mess, what appealed to the aliens?

"I promised Frill a day out and we want to dine on our favorite food. It is only found on Earth. We have had small samples from friends who brought some back to our planet."

Now they were talking her language. "What is it? Hamburgers? Steak? Fried chicken?"

"Bugs," Frill said. Her shrill voice, full of excitement, rose an octave.

"Bugs?"

"Oh, yes. We love them, but Earth is the only planet where they are found. I love grasshoppers, but Zini prefers beetles."

Janet shook her head, picked up her fishing gear, and said, "I don't want to ruin your day out. It was very nice meeting you, and you are welcome to all the bugs you can catch."

She turned and walked toward the house. She stopped for a moment and looked back. Two Leprechaun-looking aliens ran around the pond bank squealing and scooping up insects.

"Bugs," Janet muttered. "And they consider themselves to have higher intelligence."

WHEN ALIENS RETURN

Steam rose as Ruth poured coffee into her favorite Smurf mug, shook her head and parked her posterior on a kitchen chair. She tried to make little noise, although it would serve them right. Seven in the morning and they were still asleep. The television blared until long past midnight, so she had no idea when her daughter and grandson would greet the day and be ready for breakfast.

No complaining, she reminded herself. Her daughter's visits were rare and her teenage grandson's even more so.

Ruth walked to the kitchen window and stared at the empty clothesline. Trying to be quiet in your own home was ridiculous, but she guessed it was the polite thing to do. Heaven knows someone in the family needed to practice good manners.

A bright light streaked across the sky. Could it be? Her heart beat faster as she crammed her feet into shoes and ran toward the pond.

Five years ago aliens splashed down. She told no one, because she had no proof. Were they back?

Ruth stopped at the water's edge and watched the metallic orb circle the pond as it had before. It stopped, the door opened and munchkin-sized aliens scampered across a ramp to greet her.

"Zini! Frill! I'm so happy you're back."

"We didn't get lost this time," Frill squealed.

"We didn't get lost last time," her husband, Zini, replied.

Ruth laughed at the couple. "Well, I'm very glad to see you. Are you back for more bugs?" On their first visit, the aliens explained their love for a cuisine only found on Earth— bugs.

"Oh, no," Zini answered. He rubbed his beard. "Frill wants to see the King."

"The King?" These leprechaun-looking space visitors had funny ideas. "This is the United States of America. We don't have a king. The closest person to that, I guess, would be our president. But he is in Washington, D.C. You are a long way from there."

"No, no, no!" Frill jumped up and down. "I want to see the King. I want to see Elvis."

"Elvis?" How was Ruth going to tell her adorable friends that they would have better luck trying to see the president? She cleared her throat. "Frill, I'm sorry. When you were here last time, you said you had television. Didn't you hear that Elvis died?"

"Of course we heard that. Frill cried for a week," Zini answered. "But we saw a commercial last week that said Elvis was putting on a show in a place called Branson."

"I looked it up." Frill's face shone with excitement. "Branson is in Missouri! Last time we were here, you said this is Missouri. Now where is Elvis?"

Ruth looked at the excited face. She would rather shoot the Easter bunny in front of a five-year-old than break the heart of this precious little being.

"Come on up to the house and have some coffee. I'll call and find out what time the show starts."

"Great," said Frill. "Is it Starbucks? Mother said Starbucks has wonderful coffee."

"How would she know?" Zini rolled his eyes.

Ruth giggled. "No, I'm afraid it's just Folgers."

In all the excitement Ruth forgot her sleepy-headed family, until her daughter and grandson walked into the kitchen.

"Mother, who---"

"Abby, I'd like you to meet my friends, Zini and Frill." The blood drained from her daughter's face. Her mouth fell open in an unflattering gape. "Zini, Frill, this is my daughter, Abby, and my grandson, Bullet."

"Bullet?" Frill wrinkled her nose. "Like in a gun? What an odd name."

"Look who's talking," Ruth's grandson snapped.

Better head this off, Ruth thought. "I'm taking Zini and Frill to Branson to see Elvis."

"Are you crazy?" Bullet was nothing if not rude. "You can't take them out in public. Just look at them."

Ruth looked at Zini in his emerald green frock coat, with his white beard and pointed ears. She looked at Frill in her green and white polka dot dress, looking fit for a square dance.

She examined her grandson with his tongue pierced, and a piercing in his eyebrow. His hair covered the other eye and looked like it hadn't been washed in days. He wore a black tee shirt with skull and crossbones on it, and jeans with more holes than a golf course, and drooping low enough to show at least three inches of underwear.

Ruth closed her eyes and saw a vision of an overweight guy with long sideburns in a glittery white jumpsuit.

She looked again at Zini and Frill. "Hey, why not? To be honest, I think they'll fit right in," Ruth laughed. "Come on," she said to the aliens. "Let's go to Branson. The King awaits."

IDENTITY THEFT

The screen door banged mercilessly against the door jam. Molly made no effort to contain her anger, or slow the door, as she flung it open and stormed into the house.

Millicent Ivie Branstetter believed herself to be high-class society. Molly knew her to be a first-class snob. She had the misfortune of being in the same class as Millicent all through high school. After graduation, a year ago, Molly hoped never to cross paths with the wannabe socialite again.

Teenage life is rough enough, but when someone in your class also shares your name it can be miserable. Not only did they have the same first name, their last name was identical. Her mother reluctantly agreed when Millicent asked to be called Molly. In no way did she want to be mistaken for that rich, pretentious brat.

A year of leisure had not improved Millicent's disposition in the least. Molly, on the other hand, had spent the last year working double shifts at the local diner to pay for her mother's funeral.

Since her mail consisted of junk mail and bills, Molly waited until Saturday mornings to check her post office box. This morning she had the displeasure of an encounter with Millicent.

"What kind of fool doesn't have life insurance?" The conceited girl's laugh echoed in the small post office. Of course she was accompanied by two friends. Their kind always traveled in packs.

Face flushed hot with anger and embarrassment, Molly ran out of the post office. Still seething, she tossed the mail on the kitchen table.

That's when it caught her eye, an envelope with her name handwritten, not the usual stick-on mailing label. Excitement replaced anger as she ripped the envelope and opened the letter.

My Dearest Millicent, it began. Good grief, this couldn't be hers. She was nobody's 'dearest.' Flipping the envelope, she read Millicent Branstetter. That was her. Box 93. That wasn't her. Her box number was 39. Poor Mr. Whittaker, the postmaster, had given her someone else's mail.

She moaned. This letter was intended for snooty Millicent. Obviously the writer did not share her low opinion of her ex-classmate. Who on earth, besides Millicent herself, held that girl in such high esteem?

Knowing full well she shouldn't, Molly read on. *This has been the longest year of my life. Mother has offered to pay for a trip home, but I know college is proving to be more expensive than they expected.*

Molly blushed as she read how much he loved and missed her. If only it was her. The last few sentences made her blood boil. *I know you must be busy, but I thought you would write. I have tried to phone, but you're always out. Hopefully we'll connect soon. All my love, Jeffrey.*

That egotistical snob led Jeffrey around by the nose throughout their senior year. Molly never knew what he saw in her, or how the son of a farmer was allowed into her shallow, self-absorbed world. With dark brown hair and piercing blue eyes, Jeffrey Parker was very easy on the eyes, and Millicent wasn't blind. Molly concluded the superficial snob liked hanging on the arm of a good-looking guy.

Poor Jeffrey. Out of sight, he was off Millicent's list the minute he left town. She had been seen with any number of dates over the past year, and all members of her parent's country club. How could anyone be so cold and heartless? Molly shook her head. Jeffrey deserved better.

Opening a kitchen drawer, she fumbled through receipts, bills, and more bills. She finally laid hands on her mother's stationary. With pen in trembling hand she began. *Dear Jeffrey*. No, that wouldn't do. She couldn't picture Millicent calling anyone 'dear.' After shredding the first attempt, she started again. *Jeffrey, I have been very busy, but that is no excuse for my ill manners. I should have written much sooner. I promise to do better, but with all my volunteer work I'm seldom home for phone calls*. With her wages, she sometimes felt like a volunteer. Jeffrey might believe Millicent was spending time with one of her mother's charitable organizations. He would never believe she had a job. *I miss you terribly but think it very practical and selfless of you to consider the hardship a trip home could put on your parents. I have been having problems with my post office box, so I just got a new one. It's* Molly left the number blank. She would tend to that first thing Monday morning. She wanted a number that in no way resembled Millicent's. From now on, Jeffrey Parker's letters would come to her, and he would get replies.

Blushing, she signed the letter *Love, Millicent.* Folding it carefully, Molly slipped it into an envelope. It would remain unsealed until she took care of the box number. Using the return address on his envelope, she addressed the letter. Her heart raced. This was wrong. She didn't care. Jeffrey was a nice guy and didn't deserve to be ignored.

Weeks passed. Her usual routine of going to the post office only on Saturday went out the window. Molly found herself rushing to check her box daily. As the stack of letters from Jeffrey grew in her dresser drawer, they also grew more personal and passionate.

Molly found herself telling him things in her letters that she had never told anyone. She felt free to share her hopes and dreams for the first time in her life. Molly could tell Jeffrey anything, almost.

On trips to the post office, she floated on air. Molly found herself humming in public. At long last she was happy.

Then the week came when not one letter arrived. Her mind raced. Had she said the wrong thing in a letter? Was Jeffrey sick or injured? Then a horrendous thought jolted her back to reality. Had he talked to Millicent? She felt ill. What had possessed her to think she could get away with such a lie?

Time for her shift at the diner, Molly forced herself out the door. She would have preferred crawling into bed and pulling the covers over her head. Dragging herself to work, Molly had difficulty concentrating.

"Excuse me, miss, but I ordered the hot roast beef."

"I'm so sorry." Shaking her head, she picked up the plate holding a cheeseburger and headed for the kitchen. She had mixed up more orders in one day than she had the entire time she'd worked there.

Just when she thought the day couldn't get any worse, Mr. Whittaker walked in followed closely by none other than Jeffrey. They sat at a table near the window. Molly had to keep her wits together. The man she loved was clueless of her ruse. "I'll be with you in a minute."

Mr. Whittaker nodded and smiled. Jeffrey, on the other hand, looked ready to tangle with a tiger and come out on top. Molly proceeded to pour coffee at the table next to them. It was easy to overhear their one-sided conversation.

"I can't believe I let you pay for this trip. What a waste of money. I came home just to surprise her. It was a surprise all right, but not for her. She said she didn't know what I was talking about. She claims she never wrote me one single letter. How could she say that?" His fist hit the table.

Startled, Molly forced herself to approach the two men. "May I get you something to drink?"

With a twinkle in his eyes, the postmaster said, "Millicent, do you know my nephew, Jeffrey?"

"Millicent?" The young man looked up, his face a mixture of confusion and disbelief. Slowly a knowing smile crept across his handsome face. "Millicent Branstetter?"

"Most folks call me Molly." She felt her face grow hot and knew it had to be as red as the tablecloth.

"Most, but not all." Sparkles danced in his piercing blue eyes.

The bell on the door jingled as Millicent entered the diner and strutted to the table where Jeffrey sat. Pen and pad in hand, Molly stepped aside.

"Jeffrey, I've been thinking." Not bothering to acknowledge Molly's existence, the self-absorbed girl brushed her long, blond hair away from her face and continued. "Forget the nonsense about those stupid letters. I'll go out with you tonight. Pick me up at six for dinner."

The young man stood, his jawbone set firm. Taller than Molly remembered, his shirt exposed his rippling muscles. No wonder Millicent could find time in her busy social schedule. "I won't be picking you up tonight or any other night. I have a date. My uncle kept telling me there was more than one fish in the ocean, but I didn't have to go that far. There's more than one Millicent right here in town. Right, Molly?"

Pen and paper hit the floor as his strong arm went around her waist and pulled her close. Rendered speechless, Molly nodded.

"You have got to be kidding?" Millicent's shrill voice could be heard throughout the small diner.

Jeffrey's uncle erupted in laughter.

"You!" Millicent turned on the postmaster. "You stupid old man! You had something to do with this!"

Still smiling, the older man narrowed his eyes and looked squarely at his accuser. "Won't say I did or didn't. But if I did, it was the smartest thing I've ever done."

Angry, Millicent stomped out.

"I didn't think she'd ever leave," Jeffrey looked into Molly's eyes. "Now, how about dinner tonight? Pick you up at six?"

BIGFOOT'S MOTHER

A sigh slipped from Dr. Matthew Curry's lips. One more patient and he could call it a day. It was a new patient at the request of a good friend. Why had he given in to Jason's prodding?

Jason King, a family practitioner, asked him to see one of his regular patients. Unable to describe the nature of the woman's problem because she refused to confide in him, Jason assured Matthew the lady needed more help than he could provide. Being a psychiatrist, Matthew agreed to talk with her.

As he sipped his coffee, the doctor mulled over the prospect of another patient. Probably an empty nester with a mid-life crisis. Depression. Anxiety.

After twenty years in this noble profession, he dreaded going to work. His ambition to help people remained intact, but his tolerance had evaporated for folks who wanted to whine and never help themselves.

Over the past five years, going to a psychiatrist had become the 'in' thing to do. Women from the local Country Club considered it chic to talk about their feelings and be analyzed by a professional. Something once thought of as taboo was now a symbol of status.

One more patient. Might as well get it over. He pressed the button for his receptionist. "Lucy, can you step in for a minute?"

The ever-pleasant Lucy Marsh made his days bearable. With uncanny natural ability, Lucy sized up patients and gave accurate predictions on what the doctor could expect. Although Matthew had to admit, some were obvious.

"Look out," Lucy warned when bleached blonde Peggy Ann Grimes came for an appointment. "She's now a redhead. With Peggy that means one thing. She changes hair color every time she gets rid of a husband and starts trolling for a new one.

Be careful. You don't want to be number six," she chuckled.

The doctor smiled and recalled how Lucy hit the bull's eye. No sooner was Peggy in his office than her long, fake eyelashes started batting like they were swatting flies. As if that weren't enough of a distraction, it was all he could do to keep Peggy on the opposite side of the desk. He never revealed this information to Lucy, but judging from her grin, she knew.

Then there was the day Madeline Riser hobbled in. Lucy stepped in his office, closed the door, and announced, "Me Me Madeline is here."

"Lucy," he scolded.

She laughed. "You know it's true, and I can tell you right now what her problem is."

"Go ahead, Dr. Freud."

"Well, we both know she is the most vain, self-centered person to breathe oxygen."

It was pointless to try and stop Lucy. Besides, she was right.

Lucy continued. "The old gal broke her big toe and now she's walking with a limp. I'd bet my paycheck she's here to whine because she thinks everyone is talking and snickering behind her back."

"Well, are they?"

"Come on, doc. It's Madeline. Of course they are."

Being an ethical doctor, Matthew never told his receptionist she was on target again. He just winked as Madeline limped out of the office.

Matthew slid his cup to the side of the desk and braced for Lucy's diagnosis of this latest patient.

Lucy entered with no trace of her usual cheerful demeanor. She gently closed the door and spoke in a concerned voice. "Doctor, this lady really needs your help."

"Now, Lucy, they all do."

"Not like this," his receptionist insisted. "She's carrying a tremendous burden. I see it in her eyes. You have to help her. Her name is Irene Merritt. Shall I send her in?"

"Yes, please do," he replied. Curiosity made his heart race. He was anxious to meet the little lady who had managed to confound and worry Lucy.

Dr. Matthew Curry was very grateful he had his own teeth, because he would have swallowed dentures at the sight of Irene Merritt. There was nothing little about this lady. He was almost six feet tall and she looked down at him.

He swallowed hard and hoped his voice didn't quiver. "Hello, Mrs. Merritt. I'm Dr. Curry." He extended his hand. With a grip most men would envy, she shook it. "Please have a seat."

"I appreciate you squeezing me in, but I'm sorry Dr. King bothered you. He really shouldn't have. I'll be all right." Irene trembled.

"It can't hurt to get a second opinion since you're already here. Why don't you tell me what's troubling you?"

She took a deep breath and said, "It's almost Halloween."

Oh, great! Prepared for a serious problem, instead he had a grown woman with a fear of ghosts and goblins.

What happened to Lucy's intuition? She sure stumped her toe on this one.

"So, you're afraid of Halloween?" He struggled to maintain a serious face.

"Oh, not at all. I look forward to Halloween," Irene answered with a bright smile. Her expression darkened. "And I dread it."

"Well, first let's talk about why you look forward to it." Matthew hoped his face didn't reveal confusion.

"This is absolutely confidential?"

"Of course."

"Well," Irene hesitated. "Halloween is the only time my son can visit."

Another lonely empty-nester. "Does he live far away?"

"I don't think so, but I don't know. You see my Andrew is not what people consider 'normal.' He is very well known, though. He is commonly referred to as Bigfoot."

"That is rude. Many people have big feet. There's no shame in it."

"Doctor Curry, you don't understand." Irene shook her head. "My son is Bigfoot. Sasquatch."

He tried to comprehend her words, but this lady was obviously delusional. Matthew decided to play along and try to get a handle on her mental condition.

"What does that have to do with Halloween?"

"He can't come near town any other time of year. On Halloween, people just think it's an elaborate costume. He comes to the house and we have a wonderful, long visit in the garage."

"The garage?"

"I park my car in the driveway that night. The garage has the only door he can get through, and even then, he has to bend down. I've got an old mattress he sits on and we visit."

How was he going to help Irene? She believed her absurd fantasy. "Tell me why you dread Halloween."

With a faint smile, Irene said, "It is so wonderful to see my son, but the visit is never long enough. I know it will be another year before I see or talk to him again. I have these feelings every year, but this year there's something else."

"What?"

The clock on the mantel ticked away the seconds as Matthew waited for a response.

"An author has written a book titled 'My Best Friend, Bigfoot.' Since its release there has been renewed interest in searching for Bigfoot. I'm afraid for Andrew."

This woman gave 'losing yourself' in a good book new meaning. "Someone wrote a book about your son?"

"No, Doctor, she wrote a book of fiction. But some people can't tell the difference."

"Irene, that's very true." Matthew posed his next question gently. "Can you?"

Tears streamed down his patient's face. "Doctor, I have been living with reality for many years. I homeschooled Andrew because he was the height of a teenager by the time he was five. His father couldn't handle having a son who was different. He left us when Andrew was six."

Lucy was right. Irene needed help, but the perplexed doctor wondered how. Should he treat her for delusions, depression, or anxiety?

"I'm sure you've had a rough time. Being a single mother is no simple job." Perhaps stress had ignited the delusion and the recent book fanned the flame of her imagination. "We're out of time, but I'd like to see you again day after tomorrow."

Irene nodded. "I was skeptical about coming but talking has helped."

Still awake at midnight, Matthew stared out the bedroom window. A colleague once told him every doctor has one case that will test his, or her, faith in their ability. Irene was his. How had such a sweet lady lost touch with reality?

Beads of sweat formed on his brow and he sat up in bed. What if Irene was telling the truth? What if Andrew/Bigfoot was real?

Matthew ignored the tales of Bigfoot that had circulated for years, but he couldn't ignore his patient. If Bigfoot was real, he had a mother. Could she be Irene?

For the next two weeks Matthew struggled with his curiosity and the fear of feeding her fantasy. He tried to listen with an open mind.

Irene explained her mother had 'the talk' with her when she was a teenager. Not the normal talk; her mother revealed the family carried the Bigfoot gene. Her mother's brother, Earl, hadn't been seen in years. He was a Bigfoot.

She wiped tears as she described her first encounter with Earl. "Andrew was fourteen and already eight feet tall. Uncle Earl knocked on the door in the middle of the night and said, 'It's time.'"

Irene paused, took a deep breath and continued. "Somehow I knew what he meant. Andrew left with him that night to live in the Land of Bigfoot. Now I see him once a year for a few short hours. But at least he's not alone."

"How old is Andrew?"

With a mother's pride, she replied, "He turned thirty-five last month, and his height is now over nine feet."

"So he lives with your uncle?"

"Uncle Earl died a few years ago, but Andrew says there are others. He's very happy."

Matthew noted the time. "I'm sorry, but our session is over." He looked at the calendar. "Tomorrow is Halloween. Should we schedule a visit for the day after?"

"Dr. Curry, I want to invite you to my garage tomorrow night."

Without hesitation, he responded, "I would be honored."

Matthew parked his car in Irene's driveway on Halloween night. With trepidation he knocked on the garage door as she had instructed. Would he be forced to help her confront her delusion or would he come face to face with a legend?

The following February, Matthew gazed

out his office window at the blanket of snow covering the ground.

Lucy burst through the door. "I told you Irene Merritt needed help. I didn't tell you to marry her. Isn't that against the rules?"

The doctor grinned. He knew his receptionist would be full of questions after he told her to clear his calendar last week so he could elope.

"It's Irene Curry now, and she hasn't been a patient since last October. The only thing she ever needed was someone to listen."

"Doctor, this is outrageous."

He held up his hand and ceased her tirade. "Lucy, would you get me a cup of coffee?"

She made an abrupt turn and marched out.

Matthew laughed. Outrageous? What he wouldn't give to introduce Lucy to his new stepson.

FUNNY MAN

"I just don't feel funny tonight."

Jesse stared at the comedian. "We all have off days, Hank. You know the show must go on. Besides, you're the one people come to see. The funniest act in Branson."

"They come for the music, too," the funny man protested. "And tonight you'd better pick up the slack cause I'm telling you I'm not in the mood."

"What's the problem?"

"I got a good look at the crowd."

"It's a packed house. How can that be a problem?"

Hank shrugged.

Jesse slipped on his sequined jacket and slapped Hank on the back. "Ready or not, it's time to shine."

Offstage, Hank listened to the first song. No doubt about it, these guys were good. As the song came to an end, he screwed an Ozark-sized grin on his face and strutted on stage. Time for the usual routine.

"Well, good evening, Hank. How are you this fine day?" Jesse managed to sound surprised to see the comedian.

"Me? I'm having a bad day."

From the look on Jesse's face, Hank knew he was stumped. This wasn't the script and he was not good at ad lib.

Hank plowed forward. "Look at that feller in the front row." He pointed. "Hey, mister, is that your wife?"

The man nodded with a smug smile on his face.

Hank looked at Jesse and grinned. "I feel better now."

"You feel better now?" The dumbfounded look on Jesse's face was not an act.

"Yep! Just take a look at that woman. I've just had one bad day. That poor feller ain't had a good day since he got married. She put the woe in woman."

The audience roared. The man on the front row laughed. The woman smiled through clenched teeth.

Hank did feel better. That would teach his ex-wife to sit front and center.

THE FATE OF TATE

Jasper Tate lay dead as an armadillo trying to cross the road during rush hour. Becky should scream, or faint, or do something girly. Instead, she burst into laughter. The contemptible coot was long overdue for some good, old-fashioned justice, and somebody had delivered it. But who? The laughter stopped.

If she called the police, there would be an investigation. Inquiries would bring all kinds of ugly details to light. Friendships would be trashed. Families shattered. Ashamed of her relief, a tear trickled down her cheek. How had she ever allowed herself to fall for him? How could someone so mean, be so charming? Ten years ago, at the ripe old age of nineteen, she became another notch on his bedpost, and had kicked herself ever since, almost.

With jobs in short supply, Becky swallowed her pride and became a waitress at the T-Bone Café. A ridiculous name since there wasn't a T-bone on the menu.

Becky looked into the face of her boss, and for the first time did not feel intimidated. The blue eyes that once pierced her heart now stared, cold and blank, at the ceiling. He might be looking up, but unless he had a last-minute change of heart, his final destination was far from heavenly.

She grabbed a nearby tablecloth and draped it over his head. The man didn't scare her, but the dead body was a different story. A chill crept up her spine as the reality of the situation sank in. She shivered.

Startled by the ring of the telephone, Becky stepped backward and bumped into a table. Good heavens! As jittery as a cat with eight expired lives, she let the phone ring. Jasper couldn't force her to open the cafe today or any other day. She inched toward the door and locked it. A sign. She needed to put a sign on the door. Everyone in town knew Jasper would never stand for his business to be closed. You can't make money that way. She looked at the tablecloth on the floor. He would never squeeze another dime out of anybody in this town, or any other.

CLOSED FOR INVENTORY. She taped the sign to the front door. No one would question that Jasper wanted to keep track of his assets. With the blinds closed, Becky removed the phone from its holder.

"Danny, is Leon there?" She hated to drag anyone into this mess, but she trusted her brothers. "I need the two of you to come to the cafe. Come around to the back door. I'll explain when you get here."

Not wanting to answer any questions, she didn't wait for a response. Becky clicked the Off button.

Voices indicated the coffee crowd was gathering and none too happy about the locked door. "Nobody said a thing about any inventory."

She recognized Willie Hawkins's voice. It was hard to believe Willie still patronized the cafe owned by the man who devised the nastiest smear campaign in the history of Glory, Missouri. Jasper didn't want to be mayor, but he made sure Willie's brother, Ben, didn't get the job. He wanted a "yes" man in the position and never gave a thought to the havoc he created while making it happen. It was also a well-known fact Jasper wanted Ben's wife. Connie Hawkins turned him down flat, and with injured pride, he retaliated.

Rumors started without a shred of proof to back them up. Ben's wife endured all she could. She divorced him and left town with their three children. The rumors proved to be false, but not before Ben lost his wife, kids, and the election. Yes, Becky reasoned, Ben had plenty of reasons to want Jasper dead.

Karen! Becky's fingers trembled as she punched numbers on her cell phone. Please let her be running late, as usual.

"Hello."

"Karen, it's Becky." She had to make sure the cook didn't show up for work.

"Hey, I'm sorry I'm late. Is your stomach acting up again?"

"No, I'm fine." Becky blushed. "But Jasper isn't up to opening the cafe today, so we've got the day off."

"What's wrong? That tightwad would have to be at death's door not to open for business."

He wasn't at death's door, he'd gone through it. "I didn't ask any questions," Becky said. "Just glad for the day off." Positive her voice didn't sound as carefree as she wanted, Becky ended the conversation.

"Hey, sis, what's going on?"

She heaved a sigh of relief at the sound of her brother's voice. "I'm in here, Leon."

"What the devil's going on? I was fixing to work on my Mustang." Her older brother loved to tinker with cars, but that was the extent of his exertion. He would never be labeled a workaholic.

She pointed at the floor.

"When did you start covering the floor with tablecloths?"

"Jasper is under it."

"Well, that's dumb. What's he doing under there?"

"He's dead, Leon. Someone killed him."

"Who would want to do that?" Danny, her younger brother, stared at the covered lump on the floor.

Leon laughed. "Who wouldn't? Ain't a person in the county that'll miss him. His grandma, bless her sweet soul, was the only one who could tolerate him."

Jasper's grandmother raised him after the death of his parents in a car crash. A huge insurance settlement was placed in a trust fund until he was twenty-one. Becky watched, with the rest of the town, as his grandmother spoiled him. Nobody blamed her. It was a natural response to a tragic situation. But as Jasper grew older, he grew mean. He had money. He knew it, and he knew how to use it, but not in a good way.

Shock filled the town when Jasper's grandmother put the deed of her home in his name and he evicted her. She lasted one month at Pleasant Villa Senior Living Facility. Everyone believed her death was the result of a broken heart.

"I guess you'd better call the sheriff," Danny mumbled.

"I can't call Roy. He would have to arrest somebody." Becky's voice shook.

"Yeah, that's what happens when somebody gets killed."

"But do we really want one of our friends to go to jail for getting rid of the trash?"

"You can't just leave him there." Danny plopped into the nearest chair, removed his cap, and scratched his head.

"Why do you think I called you? I can't move him by myself."

"Where are we going to take him?" Danny scratched his scalp harder.

"Quit raking your head like you've got fleas," Becky scolded. "We've got to bury him where nobody will ever find him."

"Bury him?" Leon took a step backward. "People will start asking questions. He'll be missed."

"Folks may wonder where he's gone, but like you said, he won't be missed." Becky hoped her brothers would soon discover their backbones. "If his funeral was held tomorrow, mourners would have to be hired."

"But a person can't just disappear," Danny protested.

"Jimmy Hoffa did," Becky asserted.

"Jimmy's missing?" Danny's eyes widened. "I just saw him yesterday at the hardware store."

"That was Jimmy Hoefner, not Hoffa." Leon slapped his forehead.

Becky wanted to slap them both. "We can't stand around all day. Let's get rid of this body." She stooped and removed the tablecloth.

"You said he was murdered," Leon said. "Where's the blood?"

The shock of discovering Jasper's dead body caused Becky to leap to, what she considered, the obvious conclusion.

"Maybe he had a heart attack," Leon offered.

"You'd have to have a heart first," Becky scoffed.

"He didn't have a heart?" Nobody would ever mistake Danny for a Rhodes Scholar. "You can't live without a heart."

Leon cackled. "He's dead, ain't he?"

"Maybe somebody suffocated him with a pillow," Danny said. "I've seen that on TV."

"Well, on TV did the guy lie down on the floor so they could kill him?" Leon slapped his knee and laughed harder.

"He could've been taking a nap." Danny's face turned red.

"Jasper Tate taking a nap on the floor. I guess he was using the tablecloth as a blanket."

Her younger brother shrugged. "You explain it then."

First-hand knowledge told Becky that Jasper wasn't above rolling around on the floor but napping there was a different story. Fed up with the dimwitted duo, she snapped, "We don't have time to explain it. We've got to get him out of here." If they didn't get a move on, they were going to be caught with a dead body and no explanation. "We'll take him out the back door. Leon, get behind him and lift."

"I ain't ever touched a dead body." Her brother hesitated. "Well, I do throw out dead mice for momma. But that's different."

"A varmint is a varmint. Now come on," Becky urged.

Leon stepped behind Jasper's head and bent down. "I'm gonna sit him up. You grab his arms and hold him steady till I get a good hold of him around the chest."

Danny moaned.

Beads of sweat formed on Leon's brow as he raised the dead man to a sitting position.

"Hurry up. I'm gonna be sick." With a firm grip on Jasper's arms, Danny stood straddling the lower part of the corpse.

"Nobody's going to be sick," Becky ordered.

"Not even you? You've been looking puny lately."

Exasperated that Leon had chosen this particular time to become observant, she insisted, "I'm fine. Now get him out of here."

Taking a deep breath, Leon put his arms around Jasper's chest, clasped his hands together, and lifted.

"Wait!"

Startled, Leon relaxed his hold. "Do you want him out of here or not?"

"Look." Becky pointed at something on the floor.

"A peanut. So what?"

"It just popped out of Jasper's mouth. That fool choked to death on a peanut."

"Nobody killed him?" Danny was as pale as the corpse.

"Nobody killed him."

"Can we call the police now, sis?" Relief flooded Leon's face.

"Yep. We'll let the police take care of this mess," Becky answered.

"Hallelujah! We were doing a terrible job."

Becky picked up the telephone and looked at the lifeless body on the floor. She took a deep breath and exhaled. Alive or dead, Jasper Tate was trouble.

Her hand came to rest on her stomach. She knew better than to drink, but Jasper offered her a beer. One led to two. Add Willie Nelson on the radio, and they were on the road again, so to speak. One stupid night, a few short weeks ago, changed her life forever.

Her fear of fighting him for custody ended with his life. No one knew, and no one would. Her baby deserved better.

BIG GIRL BRITCHES

Kayla dreaded the night for weeks in advance. Her tenth high school reunion was a disaster. Why did she think the twenty-fifth would be any better? Why had she agreed to go?

"Honey, are you ready?"

She tensed at the sound of her husband's question. With one last look in the mirror, she replied, "Ready or not, here I come."

"We're not playing Hide and Seek." Jake laughed.

"I'd rather," she mumbled and headed downstairs.

Her heart beat faster at the sight of her husband. High school sweethearts, it seemed they'd been together forever yet only just begun.

Jake attempted conversation on their ride to the restaurant. "Do you think many will be there?"

"There weren't many to start with," Kayla said.

"Yeah, I guess nineteen isn't a big class," he chuckled. "Did I tell you how pretty you look tonight?"

"Thanks, but I'm still just plain old me."

"There's nothing plain or old about you," Jake said as he parked the car. "Now let's have a good time."

Still unsure of the whole thing, Kayla smiled and nodded. It was time to put on her big girl britches and have fun.

Seated at the table, Kayla felt silly for wasting her time being a worrywart. Everyone was being extremely pleasant.

Name tags were a life saver. She couldn't believe Randy Miller's hair loss, or Rachael McCreed's enhancement surgery.

Class president Tom Grant stood and welcomed everybody. "I guess we really should find out what everyone's been up to. Of course, you all know I'm practicing medicine in Oklahoma City. Now let's go around the room and hear what you're doing. Nancy, you can start."

Kayla cringed as one by one she heard her classmates tell of their many occupational accomplishments. It was her turn.

Tom smiled and said, "So, Kayla, are you still just a housewife?"

Barbecue wafted through the room. Her stomach churned. No, she would not give him the satisfaction of seeing her barf. The longer she looked at him, the madder she got.

Rising to her feet, Kayla ignored Jake's nudge. She had been timid throughout high school and endured a painful ten-year reunion. But tonight she was wearing her big girl britches and enough was enough.

"No, Tom, I'm not just a housewife. I never have been. I married a man, not a house. The way I like housework, any self-respecting house would have divorced me years ago."

"Honey," Jake tried to interrupt.

"No, dear. Doctor Tom wants to know what I've been doing." She smiled wickedly and continued. "Jake and I have two beautiful grown children; a boy and a girl. You know what, Tom? They let me take those babies straight out of the hospital and home. No 'practice' at all." She watched the class president's smile disappear. Good.

Being put in his place was long overdue.

"I didn't attend a university and I've never had what you would consider a prestigious job, but I have been honored to have the most important job in the world; raising our children."

Kayla smiled at the pale president. "I guess that's enough about me. Oh, and Tom, next time you see your mother, tell her I said, 'Hello.'"

THE EXECUTION

Chills ran through Penny's body as the iron door locked behind her. Fifteen years ago she never imagined herself inside a prison for any reason, much less to witness an execution.

She followed a guard into a cold, gray room, and took her place on a metal folding chair. Her gaze swept the area. A few strangers, she assumed to be reporters, scribbled on notepads. Penny kept her distance. She was sick of those vultures and their ridiculous questions.

How many times had they asked, "How do you feel?"

She ached to scream, "How do you think

I feel?"

It was cruel and ironic this should take place on her fifty-fifth birthday. But why not? She would never again enjoy the date of her birth.

Her mind traveled back to her fortieth birthday celebration. With the party over, she was loading the dishwasher when a shot rang out.

Penny ran to the living room to find her husband bleeding and lifeless on the floor. She froze. Her teenage daughter screamed and begged for her life.

The gunman's eyes were cold and calculating as he held the revolver at point-blank range and pulled the trigger, fatally shooting Missy in the head. Penny screamed and he turned the gun on her. Without hesitation he took aim.

With a look of contempt plastered on his face, he said, "Happy Birthday," and shot her in the chest.

Doctors, friends, and even her pastor tried to tell her how lucky she was to have survived the bullet. They meant well, but the last thing she felt was fortunate.

Powerless to save her husband and daughter, Penny wished many days she had been buried with them. Life as she knew it was shattered.

The joke she shared with friends before

her birthday about bracing for a mid-life crisis was no longer funny. Nothing was funny. She could not recall the last time she smiled. Then again, maybe she could.

That fateful evening before she entered the kitchen, Steve, her high-school sweetheart and husband of twenty-two years, patted her behind and said, "You get prettier every day."

The twinkle in those gorgeous blue eyes made her heart flutter. She would never gaze into those eyes again.

And Missy, her beautiful fifteen-year-old daughter. Not only was she murdered, she was robbed. She never had a first date, drove a car, went to prom, graduated high school, attended college, or even went through the teenage ritual of working at McDonalds. Penny would never watch with joy as Missy selected a wedding gown, or wipe her eyes as her husband walked their daughter down the aisle.

The defense lawyer argued diminished capacity due to drug use, but the jury found the twenty-year-old defendant guilty of two counts of first-degree murder and one count of attempted murder. After fifteen years of appeals the sentence would be carried out today.

Penny struggled with the decision to attend the execution. Once again, well-meaning friends advised her. "You should go. It will give you closure."

Closure. What a word. How could anyone think there would ever be an end to this nightmare? After all these years she jumped when a door slammed, refused to watch the news or read a paper, and relived the ordeal day and night. A peaceful sleep was rare.

Doctors prescribed sleeping and nerve medications. Penny filled the prescriptions, but never opened a bottle. No pill could erase the anguish or lessen the pain.

A guard touched her shoulder. "Mrs. Jenkins, they're bringing him in."

She stared at the tall, thin man shuffling into the room on the other side of the glass. Penny searched his face for any sign of remorse. It was useless. The expression on his face was as hard and cold as his surroundings.

The warden asked, "Do you have any last words?"

The glare of the man's eyes fell on Penny, and in a tone full of disdain he spoke two words loud and clear.

"I can't do this." Penny knocked over a folding chair as she started toward the door.

"Mrs. Jenkins, it will be over soon. Just have a seat."

"I'm not staying. I should never have

come. I don't want to see anyone else die."

"Let her out," the warden ordered.

She took one last look at the condemned man behind the glass, turned and walked to the door. She heard mumbles behind her but didn't care. The reporters could write whatever they wanted. Accustomed to being fodder for the news, Penny knew his last words would be tomorrow's front-page headline, and her reaction would be analyzed.

Her shoes clicked a steady rhythm as she hurried down the long prison hall. A lone tear escaped. She wiped it away with the back of her hand. She had to get out of this place.

Tears streamed down her face as she fumbled through her purse for keys. Seated in the car, Penny's shoulders shook as she sobbed. Her trembling fingers turned the key in the ignition and adjusted the radio to a local channel in search of news. Instead, she was tortured with mindless commercials.

She watched a handful of protestors wave their signs. They had a right to their opinion, but she wondered how their point of view might change if their family was murdered.

"At noon today, the state executed Matthew Steven Jenkins for the murder of his father and teenage sister. Jenkins also seriously wounded his mother in the brutal attack."

Penny pushed the button and silenced the radio. It was over. Her son, the last member of her family, was gone.

For years she wrote letters. He returned them unopened. She phoned the prison and requested visits. He refused to see her. Until today, the last time she saw Matthew was in a courtroom, handcuffed and shackled.

Any hope of explanation or reconciliation died with him. Penny opened the compartment between the car seats and retrieved a bottle of water. She would make good use of those medications at last.

As she reclined in the driver's seat, with the empty bottles at her feet, Penny closed her eyes. Her son's last words echoed in her mind.

"Happy Birthday."

SUNDAY BUSINESS

"Who's that coming down the lane?"

"I don't know, but if he's here for mom's fried chicken, he's out of luck," Uncle Roy laughed.

It was a hot Sunday afternoon in August of 1945. The whole family had just enjoyed dinner at Grandma Lily's. The women were clearing the table and washing dishes in the kitchen while men were sprawled in various positions on the front porch. Grandkids were running wild in the yard except for me. At twelve-years of age I was too old for such nonsense. I was almost a man.

A long lane from the dirt road led to

grandma and grandpa's house. One side of the lane was lined with blackberry bushes. The once inviting bushes appeared to wilt before my eyes, revealing nothing but briars whose only purpose in life was to snag a fellow's britches. The blackberries had been delicious earlier in the summer but had long been gone. Grandma could make one mean blackberry cobbler. It sure hit the spot with the homemade ice cream with my uncles cranked up. The afternoon sun filtered through the motionless leaves of the walnut trees on the other side of the lane revealing a good crop of nuts for the fall harvest. I could swear those walnuts were sweating. We watched the stranger approaching with mounting curiosity. His shoes were kicking up dust with every step. The Ozark's earth in August is always begging for rain.

"Do you suppose he's a salesman?" Uncle George wondered aloud.

"For his sake, I hope not. Grandma won't tolerate a peddler on Sunday." Uncle Roy laughed.

"Uncle Roy, why don't you have to go to Sunday preachin'?" I decided now was as good a time as any to ask a question that had bugged me for years.

"Delbert!" My dad snapped.

"It's okay, Charles. The boy has a

legitimate question." Uncle Roy turned his eyes from the stranger to me. "Del, when you are a young un' you don't have a choice. When you get older, you can make your own decision about Sunday preachin'. Trouble is, every Sunday I make the wrong choice."

"Not much of an excuse, if you ask me," Grandpa grumbled.

The stranger was now in the front yard and coming toward the porch. "Good afternoon, gentlemen." He did resemble one of them traveling salesmen grandma detested. It was plain to see he had shed the suit jacket long ago. The sleeves of his not-so-white and sweaty shirt were rolled up and his tie dangled out of the pocket of the jacket thrown over his shoulder. On second thought, maybe he was a preacher.

"Same to you," Grandpa replied. "Where you headed?"

"Just on my way to town and saw all the cars." The stranger took out his handkerchief, removed his hat, and wiped his clean-shaven face. To his credit, the man had a nice haircut and a good clean part. Mom was very picky about the part in a man's hair. She was so fussy with mine every Sunday you would think I was doing the preachin'.

"Would you like a glass of tea?" Grandpa

offered.

"That sure sounds good."

"Delbert, get the man some iced tea," Grandpa ordered.

Dadgum it. Why couldn't he send one of my sissy cousins after the tea? I made tracks and was back in a flash. This stranger seemed a little peculiar and I sensed this was not going to be an ordinary Sunday afternoon.

"So, Bill, don't you have a car, or are you just out for an afternoon stroll?" Uncle George asked with a grin on his face.

The man, now known as Bill, seemed only too happy to take one of grandma's best jelly glasses filled with iced tea from my hands.

"Thanks." He tipped the glass and took a long drink. "Good tea. Sweet and cold." He then turned his attention back to my Uncle George whittling on a stick. Uncle George never whittled anything in particular. He just whittled. "I don't have a car, but I'm looking to buy one. I saw all the cars parked here and hoped maybe one might be for sale." The stranger looked at the yard full of cars.

Grandma Lily gave up trying to teach the men in the family to park in the driveway. Uncle George said it was too far to walk. Dad reasoned if George could park in the yard so could he. Grandpa said it was not his problem because he parked in the car house. Uncle Roy did not care enough to bother with an excuse. Grandma just rescued the surviving rose and lilac bushes and transplanted them to the back yard. Although nobody had ever driven through the lilac bush, she reasoned it wasn't worth the risk. The bush had been a transplant from her mother's yard. The rose bush was a different story. Grandpa gave it to her on their first anniversary. It was the first and last time he ever bought her anything that resembled flowers, and she vowed those boys and their confounded automobiles were not going to destroy it.

"I reckon I'd take three hundred for my car," Dad said with a laugh.

The next words wiped the smile off dad's face in a hurry. "Which one is it?" the stranger asked.

"It's the black one," Uncle Roy piped up.

Dad gave Roy one of those looks that everybody gives Uncle Roy sooner or later. Every car in the yard was black. "It's the one closest to the car house. Come on, I'll show it to you, if you think you're interested."

"I'd like to see it. What year is it?"

"It's a 1937 Chevy."

Nobody said a word as dad walked to the

car with the stranger right on his heels. Bill was looking it over from top to bottom. There was a lot of nodding going on. He stuck his head inside. Before we knew what was happening, Dad and Bill were driving off. Grandpa said something about a test drive. Uncle George said something about the heat, and Uncle Roy chuckled and said something about Mom and her quick temper. I didn't have a clue what was going on. I was nearly grown, but I sure didn't understand grown-ups.

"It was awful hot in church this morning. I didn't think the preacher was ever going to wind down." Uncle George yawned and stretched back in his chair.

"Won't be long and you'll be complaining about your feet freezing." Grandma had stepped out of the house. She whacked George on the back of the head, and then looked squarely at Uncle Roy. "As for you, young man, it's only going to get hotter for you if you don't get your hide back to church." George and Roy were my mother's brothers. Uncle George was married to Aunt Bess and had five kids. Uncle Roy was still a bachelor and lived alone in a small house not far from grandma and grandpa.

"I meant to come this morning," Roy started.

"Don't lie to your mother." Grandpa was

still the head of the family, even if all his kids were grown.

"Where is Charles?" Grandma asked.

"Some stranger wanted to test drive his car." Uncle Roy was glad to turn the spotlight on someone else.

"Test drive whose car?" Mom had just stepped out on the porch.

"Some guy named Bill is testing out your car," Grandpa explained.

"Why would he be testing our car?" Mom looked puzzled.

"He is looking to buy a car and Charles said he would sell."

"Oh for the love of Pete, what is he thinking?" Mom did not look happy. My two uncles were grinning from ear to ear. Mom turned and went back inside, letting the screen door slam behind her. Grandma followed.

Dad and Bill returned with Bill driving. Dad got out of the car, closed the door and waved as Bill drove away in our family car.

Mom flew back out the door. "Where is that man going in our car?"

"It's his car now. He paid cash." Dad had a weird look on his face.

Mom's hands instantly went to her hips. "And just how are we going to get home? If you think I'm going to walk eight miles, you'd better think again."

At this point Grandpa decided to step in. "I'll drive you home. We probably ought to be going. I have to get back and do the milking."

"Delbert, get your sister," Mom ordered.

For five-years-old, Gracie was one big nuisance. I headed to the back yard where she was playing some sissy game with my other girl cousins. Ralphie, one of Uncle George's boys, was in the back yard with them. But he was only two years old and didn't know any better. Uncle George had another boy, but he was only six months old. I did not have a boy cousin even close to my age.

"Come on, Gracie. It's time to go home." I took her hand and led her to Grandpa's car.

Mom's baking dish would ride in my lap on the way home. She sure had a way with sweet potatoes. Even though Grandma cooked plenty, Mom would always bake something to add to the meal. She said it was only proper. I didn't know about proper, but it was good.

The ride home seemed longer than usual. Somebody was in trouble and for once it was not me. Mom rode home in silence. She was puffed up like an old bullfrog.

"What are you going to do for a car now, Charles, if you don't mind my asking?"

Grandpa hit another pothole.

"I heard old man Riley across the river has one for sale. I guess I'll see what he wants for it." Dad scratched his head. "Have you ever seen anybody carry three hundred dollars in their billfold?" He was looking at Grandpa.

"Can't say that I have? Most folks have never seen that much money at one time, much less carry it around. Where was that feller from anyway?"

"Said he was headed home to Springfield. He had been visiting family in Grovespring. He didn't say how he got there. Wouldn't you think a man with three hundred dollars in his pocket would already have a method of transportation? It's nearly fifty miles from Springfield to Grovespring. I can't believe he was walking."

"The whole mess is unbelievable if you ask me, but you didn't bother to ask me." Mom broke her silence. "Why would you just up and sell our car?"

"Like I said, who carries three hundred dollars around with them? I never thought he was serious about buying a car, and I sure never thought he had the cash on him."

We were home and Grandpa said goodbye. He had chores to do and so did we. I wanted to hang around the house, but one of my chores was getting the cows in the barn lot for milking. Dad and I always did the milking, but this night I started without him. When he did finally get to the barn his mood was very sober. It seemed best not to ask any questions.

"Delbert, you can handle the milking in the morning. I'm going across the river to see Josh Riley about a car."

I nodded.

Dad left early the next morning. We lived on a hill overlooking our bottom field bordering the Osage River. In August a man could wade across the Osage in several places, but during the spring rains our bottom field would be flooded. There was no bridge nearby to cross the river. By road, old man Riley's place was several miles, but a straight shot across the river. I wanted to go with dad, but mom was busy taking care of Gracie, the chickens, and canning the last of the green beans. Somebody had to milk the cows.

The morning chores went as smoothly as chores can. That cantankerous old Angus cow tried to kick me, but I was too fast for her. If only I could break her of that bad habit. I can't count the number of times she has knocked over the milk bucket. Looking toward the river there was no sign of dad. I gathered the eggs and took a dozen to the widow lady living half a mile down the road. She usually gave me cookies, but I was in a hurry to get home today. There was still no sign of dad.

Lunchtime came and went. Mom kept looking out the kitchen window that faced the river. She turned her attention to a quilt she had in the frame. Dad said it took up too much space in the living room. She said he liked to stay warm in January and their old quilt was worn out. She got the last word.

Mom hollered and woke me from my nap in the hay loft. It was time to start the evening milking. There was still no sign of dad.

He came walking down the hill in front of our house just as I locked the cows in the lot. Mom came out to meet him. "Did you buy a car?"

"Sure did. I got a pretty good deal on it, too." Dad smiled.

"So, where is it?" Mom asked.

"It's sitting on top of the hill."

Sure enough, there it sat. The road ran along the top of the hill in front of our house. "Well, what is it doing up there?"

Dad's smile vanished. "It's got two flat tires."

"You have got to be joking. Tell me you are joking. How can you possibly call that a good deal? Do you have any idea how hard tires are to get these days? What are we supposed to do now?"

"I don't know, dear. I guess we just aren't supposed to have a car right now," Dad answered.

"That's what you get for doing business on Sunday. I guess good sense is something 'we' don't have either." Mom just kept mumbling under her breath as she walked toward the chicken house.

"What did she say, Dad?"

He just laughed and answered, "I guess we aren't supposed to know that. I'm just thankful the only neck she's wringing tonight belongs to a chicken."

'Dear' Season

Jeb shivered as he climbed into his treestand. Why hadn't he stayed there? Why had he taken a break from hunting and gone home for lunch?

Not one single deer made its presence known all morning. Taking a break for lunch seemed like a good idea. The long walk to the farmhouse gave him a chance to stretch his back and legs. His stomach growled, reminding Jeb he had skipped breakfast. The alarm didn't go off and he overslept thirty minutes. Not a good beginning for the opening day of deer season.

An odor permeated his nostrils the

second he opened the back door. Three days ago it had been a pleasant aroma. But after three days, the smell of leftover stew turned his stomach. This morning couldn't get any worse.

In anger, he threw his heavy-duty thermos across the kitchen. His wife stepped into the room just in time for the thermos to whack her right between the eyes.

Doris hit the floor with the loudest thud he'd ever heard. This morning had just gone from bad to deadly.

Kneeling beside his poor wife, Jeb moaned. "Why did you have to warm up stew again? Why did you have to walk into the kitchen?" He buried his face in his hands. "Why did I have to lose my temper again?"

He yelled at Doris daily, but had never physically hurt her. After thirty-five years of marriage it came to this. An accident. But who would believe him? His bad temper had earned him quite a reputation.

Enough self pity. He picked up his wife's lifeless body and carried her out the door. He wished she'd made good on her promise to lose twenty pounds. Thankful they had finally indulged and bought a Gator, he laid her in the bed and wiped his forehead. Between nerves and carrying Doris, he had worked up a sweat. In the garage, he grabbed a shovel and laid it beside his wife.

Driving through the woods, Jeb could not believe how this day had gone. He knew he needed to get a grip. After all, it hadn't been a banner day for Doris either. The least he could have done was cover her with a blanket. It was too late now. He wasn't going back.

The Ozark's woods are quite spectacular in the fall. This year had been no different, but most of the leaves were now on the ground.

Jeb stopped the Gator and lifted Doris out. He placed her under an old elm tree and covered her with a few leaves.

Exhausted from emotion, he climbed into his treestand to rest a while before digging her grave. Jeb shivered. Why hadn't he stayed there?

He sat on the padded seat and exhaled. His eyes scanned the surrounding woods. This time he wasn't looking for deer. Although he had posted 'No Trespassing' signs, he knew some people paid no attention. Today would not be a good day for uninvited visitors.

A sob rose in his throat as Jeb's gaze moved to the spot where he had placed Doris. Where's Doris? Her body was gone. How?

He scrambled out of the treestand. In the time it had taken him to ascend the tree, some varmint made off with Doris. This was not the plan.

Jeb slapped his forehead. What was the plan? Who plans to kill their wife with a thermos bottle?

Running into the woods, he shouted, "Doris, where are you?"

A harsh realization stopped him in his tracks. Doris couldn't answer. He had to find her. She deserved better than this. She deserved a burial.

"Hey, Jeb, any luck?"

He turned so fast he lost his balance. His neighbor, Rick, grabbed his arm. "Easy there, Jeb. Are you okay? You're as white as a stripe down a skunk's back."

"I'm fine. Just didn't hear you walk up. Guess I was daydreaming again." Jeb hoped his nosy, trespassing neighbor bought the lie.

Rick was the neighbor in a league of his own. 'No Trespassing' signs didn't apply to him. He went wherever he wanted. He had no regard for the law. Rick hunted before, during, and after deer season. His favorite hunting was done after dark in his truck with a spotlight.

"I saw a couple of does, but they were running. So, have you had any luck?"

"No. I haven't seen a thing." Jeb began to sweat again.

"You sure you're feeling okay? You don't look too good. I can call Doris." Rick whipped out his cell phone.

"There is no need to bother Doris. I'm fine. Just not as young as I once was." Jeb wished this neighborly nuisance would go away.

"Nice weather for opening day," Rick stated. A puzzled look crossed his face. "Hey, where's your gun?"

"Didn't feel like shooting anything today," Jeb answered. "Just thought I'd sit out here a while."

"I never heard of a hunter going to the woods on opening day without a gun." Rick walked off shaking his head.

Doris. Jeb had to find Doris. He searched the woods until the sun went down. Not a sign of Doris. Defeated, he started the Gator and drove back to the farmhouse.

Lights shone in the windows. Could it be? Of course it could. He hadn't checked her pulse. He had assumed the worst. Hallelujah!

Jeb burst through the door. He couldn't wait to apologize and beg her forgiveness. An enticing aroma filled the air, reminding Jeb he hadn't eaten all day.

Doris bustled about the kitchen as if

today was just like any other. She had cooked a feast for the man who gave her one whopper of a black eye. Jeb would never understand women. But he was not complaining.

Starved, he sat down to a meal of fried chicken, mashed potatoes, gravy, corn, and homemade rolls. His growling stomach drowned out his conscience. Instead of shoveling out an apology, he began shoveling in food, unaware that Doris was not eating.

"These potatoes taste different. Did you use a new spice?"

"No, just the usual."

Jeb sighed. "After the day I've had, I wouldn't care if you'd poisoned the food. I'd die happy knowing you are alive and well and I couldn't ask for a better last meal." His laugh turned into a moan. He grabbed his throat and fell to the floor.

Doris smiled, "I'm so glad I finally made you happy."

MOVING DAY

“What on earth was she doing with this rusted piece of iron in the china cabinet?”

“Beats me. But you know Mom. She was a packrat.”

Jake lowered his head as he listened to his grown children packing away his belongings. No longer able to stay by himself, his children had convinced him to move to a senior facility. There were numerous drawbacks to this move, but one of the biggest was downsizing. There simply was no room for what Jake and his late wife had accumulated over fifty years of marriage.

"Does it go in the junk pile?"

"Looks like junk to me."

A tear rolled down Jake's weatherworn face. Their children had no idea what they were tossing out. He closed his eyes and time melted away. He could see that fifteen-year-old tomboy on her little red tractor.

Only fifteen himself, Jake worked for her father hauling hay during the summer. It was hard work, but in those days if you wanted money, you had to work. Mom and Dad didn't give handouts.

He always knew she would be in the field when he got there. Her and that little red Farmall. She would be there till the last bale was stacked in the barn. Weighing less than a hundred pounds, she couldn't toss the bales around, but could stack the hay in the loft. After riding the tractor all day wearing a tee shirt and shorts, she would pull on a pair of old jeans and help put the hay in the barn. None of this work required shoes. She seldom wore shoes in the summer, but kept an old pair tied to the gearshift of her tractor. She said they were there "in case of emergency."

The piece of iron now casually being discussed was also a staple on the tractor. On rare occasions he had watched her use it to crank start the cantankerous piece of machinery.

With all its flaws and mechanical problems, she loved that little tractor. With all her flaws and housekeeping shortcomings, he had loved her.

While other girls were playing with dolls and learning to cook, his future wife was raking hay, milking cows, or sitting on her granddad's pond bank catching fish with a cane pole and worms.

This was a side of their mother his children never knew and could not appreciate. To them, she was just Mom. She never worked outside the home, but hated being called a housewife. He smiled as he recalled her words. "I did not marry a house. I married a man."

It was a good thing she was not united in marriage to the house. The poor thing would have divorced her years ago. She took her own sweet time getting around to the housework. She openly despised dusting, mopping, sweeping, and all other forms of menial labor around the house.

His wife loved being outdoors. The same woman who hated using a broom, loved holding a rake in autumn. He could not count the times he had come home from work and witnessed piles of leaves and giggling grandchildren. She also loved gardening. He never understood why she enjoyed picking beans or pulling weeds in the heat of the day. Maybe it had something to do with her childhood, when being outdoors was the only life she knew.

Without knowing it, Jake had taken a considerable risk marrying that tomboy. While she could drive circles around any man on that tractor, she was inept, to say the least, in the kitchen. The first few years of their marriage, he thought he might starve. One of her favorite foods was new garden potatoes and white gravy. While she could grow and cook the potatoes, the gravy was another story. He watched in agonizing sympathy as she tried over and over again to make gravy that even halfway resembled her mother's.

One thing he had always admired about his wife was her tenacity. If she were determined to do something, then sooner or later it would get done. Her cooking finally and steadily began to improve. What he wouldn't give to smell smoke coming from the kitchen and taste that lumpy white gravy again. He swallowed hard.

This move was going to be harder to digest than anything his wife had ever cooked.

Jake opened his eyes. "I'll take that." He took the piece of iron from his son.

"But Dad, you don't have room for junk like this."

"I appreciate all your help, but you could be a little more respectful of our 'junk'." Jake's annoyance was loud and clear in his voice.

"Now, Daddy, we talked about this. You can't keep everything."

Oh, lovely. His daughter had put on the kid gloves.

"I am not asking to keep everything. I am asking for a little respect."

"Daddy, you know we respect you. But that hunk of metal is worthless. What in the world is it doing in the china cabinet anyway?"

"That piece of iron was more valuable to your mother than any piece of china. It was all she had left of something very dear to her childhood."

"I don't understand." His daughter looked puzzled.

"I know you don't, and that's sad. There are a lot more things in this house that are going to seem ridiculous, because you never took the time to get to know your mother."

"Now you are just being silly. We knew her. She was Mom." His son was obviously losing patience with his old man.

"Sure she was Mom. But before she was your mother, she was my wife. And before that, she was somebody's daughter. You don't know beans about that person. You never knew the girl who could straighten a rake tooth with a hammer. The girl who could kill a chicken but had no idea how to cook it. The girl who would rather fish than eat. You just knew Mom, and sometimes I don't think you really knew her."

After rendering his grown children speechless, he felt somewhat guilty. "Your mother put a lot of miles on her little red tractor and that crank is all she had left of it. Your grandpa sold the tractor after we got married, but somehow the crank was left behind. It has resided in Mom's china cabinet ever since. If a piece of iron could talk, you would hear some wild tales. But it can't talk, and your mother is gone, so I guess now it is just a piece of junk."

"I'm sorry, Dad. We didn't mean to be disrespectful." There was sadness in his daughter's gentle words.

"It's okay, really. You are not the first to overlook your mother until it's too late. What I know about my own mother's childhood would fit in a teaspoon. She never talked about it, and I was too busy with my own life to ask. It didn't seem important until it was too late. Speaking of late, you guys are never going to get this house packed up if you don't stop indulging an old man and his memories."

"I'll get the cookies and something to

drink. We are long overdue for a trip down memory lane." Jake's daughter left for the kitchen.

"Sounds to me like a family vacation. Dad, I want to hear about your teen-age years." His son took the piece of rusting iron from Jake's hands. "This is going home with me."

A DINNER TO REMEMBER

Hank Winslow scowled as he hung the ridiculous portrait on the bare wall. Ballerinas dancing by a lake. His wife, Myra, refused to buy the picture of dogs playing poker. Maybe she was right on that one, but he saw nothing wrong with the painting of children wading in a stream. Oh no, she had to have the ballerinas. Said it would add a touch of class to their home. He was consoled by the fact the painting would only be there on rare occasions. Tonight was one of them.

Tonight they would meet the girl who had captured their son's heart and started a very uncivil war in their home.

Although they had only heard about Garrett's girlfriend, Hank had heard enough. He never thought his son would betray his upbringing, but he had. Hank placed the blame on that fancy college. He tried to tell Myra their son could learn all he needed to know right there on the farm. But there's no reasoning with a hard-headed woman. He had the upper hand until Garrett got a full scholarship. Money had been his best argument. With that obstacle removed, the fight was over.

Hank reminded himself daily that his son was the first in the family to attend college and would have a better life. He figured the boy would kick up his heels, date some girls, and have a good time. He never expected this.

Myra was taking the news of Garrett's girlfriend much better than he, for now. Face to face over the dinner table might be a different kettle of fish. Hank slapped his forehead. He'd forgotten the mounted bass over the dining room door. Better get that down.

With all the care of a mother tending a newborn, Hank placed his prize fish on a shelf in the bedroom closet. No highfalutin' city girl could be worth this much trouble. It would take a week to get things back to normal. He closed his eyes and hoped

Natalie didn't visit often, or better still, that his son would come to his senses.

"Hank, would you set the table?"

With more than a hint of sarcasm, Hank asked, "Where do you want me to set it?"

He watched his wife place her hands on her hips. A beautiful woman with a handsome figure, Myra was the delight of his life. Why couldn't his son find a nice girl like his mother?

"You know exactly what I mean. Get some plates and silverware and set the table."

"How would I know what you mean? We've rearranged the whole house."

The stern look on her face told Hank he was pushing his luck. "You'd better rearrange your attitude before Garrett and Natalie arrive."

"Just what else am I going to have to change for this girl?"

"Your clothes."

Hank watched his wife disappear into the kitchen. He looked down and took inventory. His faded overalls had a rip below the knee. Blasted barbed wire got him again. He hated to admit it, but Myra was right. He should change.

He placed the last fork on a cloth napkin and headed upstairs to make himself presentable. What he wouldn't give to skip the whole mess and hit the recliner.

As he buttoned his best Sunday shirt, Hank wondered how Garrett got involved with a girl like Natalie. Myra had reminded him time and again not to judge someone they'd never met. But who did she think she was fooling? He could hear the apprehension in her voice. This would be a meal to remember, if you could call it a meal.

"Hank, they're here," Myra called out.

"Guess who's coming to dinner," Hank mumbled. Attitudes are more difficult to change than clothes. He plastered a smile on his face and marched down the stairs with all the enthusiasm of a prisoner on his way to the electric chair.

"Hey, you look sharp." Garrett slapped him on the back. "Dad, this is Natalie."

Hank extended his right hand. "Nice to finally meet you," he said and marveled at the girl's strong grip.

"Garrett has told me so much about you and Mrs. Winslow and your farm. I couldn't wait to get here."

Probably couldn't wait to start the great reformation. Hank gritted his teeth and kept smiling.

With interest and more than a little amusement, Hank watched his wife exchange pleasantries with the girl.

"Mom, do I have time to show Natalie around the farm before supper?"

"You've got thirty minutes," Myra said.

Hank didn't want to like this girl, but she made it difficult. Easy on the eyes, a smile to melt ice, and no anemic handshake. If only she weren't . . . .

"Dad, old Mollie is showing her age." Back from their tour of the farm, the lovebirds strolled through the yard and onto the front porch arm in arm.

"I'll bet she wagged her tail at the sight of you."

A fixture on the farm, Garrett's black and tan hound had to be the laziest animal around, although Mollie could muster enthusiasm for eating and hunting. Hank wondered if Natalie knew how much his son loved to hunt, or if the subject had even been mentioned. He followed the happy duo into the house.

"You have some good-looking livestock, Mr. Winslow," Natalie said with a smile.

The girl was so pretty and chipper she almost sparkled. If only she weren't...

"Looks like some are ready to sell." Garrett tossed his cap on the coffee table and flopped down on the couch.

"I'd better see if your mom needs a hand in the kitchen." Hank left the room before his son could say anything else. He slammed through the kitchen door. "What is wrong with that boy? We are doing our best and he wants to talk about taking cattle to market."

"Calm down, honey." His wife filled a basket with warm breadsticks. "It'll be over soon. Just behave yourself."

"I'm trying, but your son is not helping."

"Oh, he's *my* son today." Myra snickered. "Just keep trying to put your best foot forward."

"I just hope to get through supper without sticking both feet in my mouth."

"That makes two of us. Now go tell the kids the food is ready. It's time to eat."

Hank looked at the table and snorted. "If you can call that food." He caught, but ignored, the disapproval in Myra's expression.

Seated around the table they munched on salads like a bunch of ravenous rabbits.

"Hey, Dad, what's up with the ballerinas in the living room?"

"Mom wanted to do a little re-decorating. Spruce the place up."

"But what about —"

"Natalie, would you like more iced tea?" Myra interrupted.

"No, thank you."

"And where did your big —"

"Are we all ready for the main course?"

Myra pushed her chair away from the table and hurried into the kitchen. She returned with two plates and placed one in front of Natalie and the other in front of Garrett.

"Be right back." She smiled and gathered the salad plates. "Looks like we need more bread."

Hank sat back and watched his wife flit through the kitchen door and come back with two more plates. One for him and one for herself. She also balanced a basket of breadsticks with the skill of a top-notch waitress.

As she settled into her chair, Hank smiled. His wife in all her preparation, had not noticed, or chose to ignore, the dumbfounded look on Garrett's face.

"What in the world is this?"

Hank chuckled as his son voiced an opinion he shared.

"It's Eggplant Parmesan," Myra replied with an under confident smile.

"When did you start eating eggplant?"

"Today," Hank laughed. Maybe this meal would be more enjoyable than he anticipated.

"Have you guys been to the doctor? Is somebody sick?" Concern was plastered on Garrett's face like mud on a pig.

"We're fine, honey," Myra answered. "It never hurts to try something new."

Hank watched his son push the food around his plate. "C'mon, son, if I'm gonna try it, you can, too."

"I'll try it, but it's not my thing. Sorry, Mom." Garrett frowned. "I promised Natalie a good home-cooked meal."

"This is home-cooked," Myra protested.

"You know what I mean. Meat and potatoes."

"Garrett, your mother was trying to respect Natalie's beliefs," Hank reprimanded their son.

"What does Natalie have to do with us eating eggplant?"

"You said she is a practicing vegetarian," Myra wailed in defeat.

"Is that why your trophy buck has been replaced by ballerinas and your mounted bass is gone?" Before Hank could answer, Garrett turned to his mother. "Mom, when are you going to start wearing your hearing aid? I didn't say Natalie was a practicing vegetarian. I said she is practicing to be a veterinarian."

The laughter subsided and Hank looked at the beautiful girl seated beside their son. Based on misinformation, he had formed a dislike for someone before meeting her. He now realized the only thing he didn't like in this room was the eggplant on his plate.

RECYCLED

With aluminum at an all-time high, Karen Whitaker searched the ditches near her country home for discarded cans. At the age of forty, she was known as the 'can lady', but didn't care. Every little bit helped since she was laid off at the factory over six months ago.

Karen and her husband, Russell, were content to eke out a living on their small farm the only way they knew— hard work. Some folks stood in the Wal-Mart parking lot with cardboard signs waiting for handouts. Not them. Sure, they had their rainy-day savings account, but she didn't see a cloud in the sky.

Taught at an early age "if you don't work, you don't eat," Karen took it to heart. She planted a garden and managed to can enough to get through the winter. Cooking for two doesn't take much. She longed to cook for more, but it wasn't meant to be.

Tears mingled with sweat as she swatted a bee and put another can in the burlap sack. Some pain never goes away. She hadn't understood the anguish of her adoptive parents until faced with the same plight.

Focused on her skyrocketing career, Karen's 'real' mother placed her for adoption at birth. The woman tried to reconcile with her daughter many years later, but Karen couldn't forgive. She gave thanks for the people who raised her. They would always be her parents.

Every Saturday night the locals partied at the bridge. Anxious to get to the creek, Karen picked up the pace. After they guzzled their paychecks, beer cans littered the ground. Thank heavens Russ never wasted his hard-earned money like that. She might have been inclined to knock a knot on his hung-over head.

She pushed her wheelbarrow down the dirt road to the bridge. Beads of sweat trickled down her forehead. Wiping them away, she grabbed an empty sack. Today was going to be another scorcher.

Her bag was half-full when a strange noise caught her attention. A cardboard box wiggled in the ditch. "People are so cruel," she snapped and headed toward the noise.

"What kind of person dumps an animal in a box in this heat?" Then she noticed the box wasn't closed. "Well, what kind of animal doesn't have sense enough to crawl out of the oven?"

She stepped into the ditch and the sound became distinct. Karen gasped and tears flowed as she gently removed the baby from the box. A girl. The precious thing couldn't be more than a day old.

After three miscarriages, Karen had prayed and prayed for a baby. Never did she imagine God would answer in this way.

The hot and dirty infant wiggled and cried in her arms. The poor little girl needed fed. She needed a bath. She needed clothes. How could anyone abandon a baby?

"Don't cry, angel." Trembling hands pulled the baby close and she gave the box a swift kick. Not even a blanket. "You deserve so much better and I promise you'll have it as soon as we get home."

Forget the wheelbarrow. Russell could come for it later. With the newfound bundle in her arms, Karen began making mental preparations as her feet hurried down the dusty road.

The baby quilt, made with happy anticipation and then stored out of sight with sorrow, would finally be used. There was so much to do.

Russ was bent over their '85 Chevy pick-up when Karen hurried into the yard.

"Find much junk today?"

"One person's junk is another's joy. Come and see."

With wide eyes, Russ stared at the baby.

"Can you believe anyone would toss out a child like garbage?" Karen rubbed a finger across the tiny cheek.

"I'll call the sheriff."

"You'll do no such thing." Defiance filled each word.

"Honey, we have to report this."

"No, we don't. We don't have to report anything. They'd just put her in a foster home. She already has a home. With us."

"Karen, be sensible. It's a baby, not a dog or cat. How will we explain suddenly having a baby?"

"People have babies every day. I haven't been to town in months. We'll just say we were finally blessed with a child. That's not a lie."

"And just where will we say this miracle baby was born?"

She glared at her husband. Why couldn't he just accept the blessing they'd been given? "If anyone asks, we'll say it was a home birth."

"Are you serious? You intend to keep her?"

"Hey, why not? Not only do I intend to, I am going to." Karen kissed the tiny forehead. "Come in the house. I'll make a list of what you need to get in town."

"You want me to buy baby stuff?"

"Just basics. Formula and bottles and diapers."

Russ opened his mouth, but she stopped his protest. "I can't go to town. I just had a baby."

A week passed and the tiny farmhouse had become a home for three. Karen mulled over names for their little blessing and finally decided on Melinda Joy. Melinda after the woman who raised her with unconditional love, and Joy because of the delight that filled their lives. They would call her Joy.

Afternoon sunlight danced on the lace curtains as Karen rocked Joy in the living room. A knock at the door interrupted the serenity.

Karen's heart pounded when she opened the door and saw Sheriff McCann.

"Afternoon, Karen."

"Hello, Bob. This is a surprise." She fumbled for words. "Would you like to come in?"

"Yes. Is Russell around?"

Her heart sank. He knows. But how? How much does he know?

"He's out back. I'll get him."

Fresh from tinkering with a cantankerous lawnmower, Russell wiped grease on his jeans and stretched out his hand to greet the sheriff. "Hello, Bob. What brings you out this way?"

"Wish I could say it was a social call." The sheriff paused, and then added, "I'm afraid this business is not pleasant."

"I told you we should've called him."

Karen winced, but held her ground. "We don't know why he's here. Why don't you let him tell us before you step in over your boots?"

The sheriff's nervous smile did nothing to reassure, and his next words confused her.

"I got called to Barker's Grocery. Old man Barker caught a girl trying to steal food. She was only fifteen and looked like she hadn't eaten in days. She collapsed at the Police Station and was taken to the hospital."

"I'm sorry for the poor thing, but what

does that have to do with us?" Karen carried the sleeping baby to the crib Russell made years ago.

"The doctors say she recently had a baby, but she won't talk. I'm guessing she dumped it, and if I'm not mistaken, you found it."

The color drained from Karen's face. Her chest ached. This was too much. Russell took a step toward her, but she put up her hand. "I'm okay, honey."

Her blue eyes darkened. "Yes, I found Joy in a cardboard box. Not even a blanket wrapped around her. It's a thousand wonders she survived. But she's not leaving here without her supplies. I'll go pack a bag for you."

"Leaving here?" A look of surprise covered the sheriff's face. "I'm not here to take the baby."

"You're not?"

"Good grief, no. I don't want to make trouble for that little one or you. I just wanted to clear things up."

"You're gonna let us keep a baby when you know it ain't ours?" Russell broke his silence.

"We don't have many foster parents in the county and with the government cutbacks, we aren't getting any more. You need to get a lawyer and make this a legal adoption."

"What about the girl in the hospital?" Russell scratched his head.

"She doesn't have any family. Got pregnant and ran away from her last foster home. I'll have to charge her with child endangerment and maybe attempted murder." He shook his head. "It's ugly business. These are the days I hate my job."

"Does she have a name?" Karen asked.

"Elizabeth Walker, but I probably shouldn't be giving out that information."

"Don't worry, Bob. There is a lot of rule bending going on around here," Russell shook his hand.

The sheriff sighed, walked out the front door and plodded to his car.

"You keep an eye on Joy. I'm going to the hospital," Karen announced. "I want to see what kind of person dumps a baby like yesterday's trash, and I'm going to see to it she doesn't cause us any trouble."

"Karen, we can't afford a lawyer."

"We won't have to." With more determination than thunder after lightning, she marched from the room and readied herself for a hospital visit.

The stench of antiseptic stung her nostrils as Karen hurried down the long hospital corridor. This would be a short, one-sided visit.

She shoved through the door of the hospital room prepared to unleash the wrath of the wronged on a heartless individual. She stopped short.

Elizabeth Walker looked small lying in the bed. The cruel, heartless individual Karen wanted to shred with words was a mere child. Big blue eyes, swollen from crying, stared at Karen.

"Are you another doctor?" The voice quivered.

"No, I'm a visitor."

"You got the wrong room. Nobody here but me."

"I'm here to see you."

The girl wiped strands of brunette hair from her face. "Why?"

This was not the visit Karen had planned, but she forged ahead. "I understand you had a baby."

"I gave it away." The defiance in her voice was unmistakable.

"Gave it away?" She might be a child, but Karen's tolerance was thin for bad actions and attitude. "You dumped the baby."

"Lady, I don't know who you are, and I don't care. I gave my baby to the can lady."

Karen gasped and sank into the visitor's chair.

"Hey, are you sick or something?"

"Have you ever seen the can lady?" This was not going at all the way Karen expected.

"Only from a distance. I was hiding out in an old abandoned house near that creek where she goes every Monday. Never talked to her. But I knew she'd find my baby and take care of it."

Karen swallowed the growing lump in her throat. "Yes, I did."

The girl's eyes widened. "You're the can lady?"

With a faint smile, Karen replied, "Yes, that's me. Now what were you doing hiding in the old Wilson house?"

"I run off from my foster folks. Ain't got family. I couldn't raise a baby. Are you going to take care of her?"

"That's the plan." Karen studied the child. What would become of her? The girl needed someone. "You really have no family?"

"My folks were killed in a car wreck. The only family I have is living with you."

A decision this big should be discussed with her husband, but Karen knew Russell's heart as well as she knew her own. "I think you need to come and stay with us, too," Karen stated.

The girl recoiled and tears rolled down the pale cheeks. "I'm not ready to be a mother. I can't take care of a baby."

"I don't expect you to be her mother. You need a mom yourself. If you will let us, Russell and I would like to adopt both of you."

The teenager burst into tears. "What good will that do? I'm headed for jail."

"You just rest and let me handle it."

"Can you do that?"

With a determined voice Karen assured the girl, "I know someone who can."

Karen stared at the sign on the brick building.

SUSAN GENTRY ATTORNEY AT LAW

She had never asked the woman for anything. Today was the day. She marched past the secretary and into the attorney's office. "Hello, Mother. I need your help."

ONE MAJESTIC OAK

Austin grimaced at the sight of the pickup coming down the long driveway. A fog of Oklahoma dust followed. Cody McCall was a nice enough fellow, but since lightning struck his only shade tree, he was obsessed. With trees, of all things.

"Daddy, Mr. Cody's here." Mollie kicked the soft dirt in the flower bed she was tending. Her little garden didn't amount to much, but kept her occupied, and Austin reckoned that was a good thing for a seven-year-old. Weeds outnumbered the scrawny plants, but Mollie didn't mind. She liked playing in the dirt.

"Morning, Austin." Cody climbed out of the red Chevy truck, ran his finger down the dust-covered side, and shook his head. "I can't keep this thing clean. You gonna break some horses today?"

"Yeah, I'm gonna try and ride Spirit later. That horse is living up to its name. I've got hay to bale first. The horses can't eat dust this winter. What are you up to?"

"Just got new tires put on the truck."

"Bet that hurt the wallet."

"Hurts my feelings every time I have to shell out money, but it had to be done. Been putting it off so long I was beginning to worry I might have to change a flat. Ain't got time for nonsense like that."

"What kind of nonsense do you have time for?"

"Anything but tire changin'."

"Ain't that the truth." Austin laughed. "How's the family?"

"Doris is busy canning beans and Jed's busy tormenting her."

Austin nodded. If human energy could be harnessed, Doris and Cody's six-year-old son, Jed, had enough to light up the house, and then some.

"If lightning hadn't got my shade tree, I could have fixed him up with a tire swing. That would've kept him busy for a while." Cody pulled off his hat, wiped his forehead, and then put it back on with a tug. "That old oak of yours is perfect for a swing."

Before the cowboy could object, Cody opened the tailgate and pulled out a worn tire. "Hey, Mollie, here's a present for you."

The barefooted little blonde abandoned her flowers. "A present for me?"

"All you need is a rope and you'll have a tire swing with your daddy's help."

"Thanks, Cody." The man might have good intentions, but the last thing Austin needed was another chore. He was less than grateful.

"Do you know how lucky you are to have that beautiful oak?"

Here we go again. More tree talk. "Yeah, it's a pretty tree," the weary friend agreed.

"It ain't just pretty. It's majestic." The forlorn look Austin knew all too well covered Cody's face. "I don't know why the lightning had to take my tree. I'd have rather lost my house."

"Cody, that's just ridiculous. You don't mean that." The man was carrying this obsession too far.

"Do you know how long it takes for a tree to grow? My tree was over a hundred years old. Why, I can't replace it in my lifetime. I could have a new house built in just a few months."

Austin decided this argument wasn't

worth the fight. If Cody wanted to mourn the loss of a stupid tree, who was he to stop him? Austin wished the man could be stoic. It was obvious he was not a believer in silent suffering.

"I'd better get on home. Doris should have lunch ready."

"Thanks for the tire. I'll put it up first chance I get."

Austin watched Cody's truck disappear into a cloud of dust. Rain was sorely needed. He hoped to get his hay in the barn first, but at this point he would take rain whenever it came. Then again, what choice did he have?

"Daddy, Momma's comin'."

The girl's eyes were better than his. All he saw was more dust. Beth left for the feed store over an hour ago. She should be home anytime, and then he could head to the field.

"Daddy, are you really gonna fix me a tire swing?"

Blast Cody McCall and his ideas. Austin looked down at the daughter he adored. Her smile soothed his irritation. "When I get time, and find some rope, we'll fix up a first-rate swing. But right now, I've got feed to unload and hay to bale." He rubbed his chin and tried to look thoughtful. "It may be a few days. I have to get some rope in town."

"Momma, guess what?"

Austin watched the bare feet kick dust as the little girl ran to greet her mother and report on Cody's gift. This was the family he always wanted, but never thought he'd have.

Austin, raised on the adjacent ranch, watched the happy girl-next-door transform after the loss of her parents. She inherited the stress of maintaining the family property. At eighteen, Beth struggled to finish high school and work the ranch. She kept her battle private, but Austin witnessed, firsthand, the toll it demanded of her.

The same could not be said for Bobby Jackson. The high school football star never gave her a second look. He had a full ride to the University of Oklahoma, until he got the bright notion to compete in the Mexican Sweat at the local rodeo.

A card table and four chairs were placed in the center of the arena. Four contestants, or suckers in Austin's opinion, sat in the chairs while a bull was released. The person who managed to stay in their seat while the wild bull circled, butted and threw the table, won a hundred bucks.

After a couple of beers, Bobby took his seat in the ring and boasted that he would collect the prize money as soon as the others ran like scared little girls.

Austin usually ignored this part of the rodeo and spent his time in mental preparation for bronc-riding. But that night curiosity drew him to the arena. It wasn't every day he had the opportunity to watch a puffed-up football star mentally tackle a Brahma bull. The bull had the advantage in more ways than one. Austin expected to enjoy seeing Bobby run from the arena. Instead, the fool refused to leave his seat.

With a horrified crowd looking on, the bull tossed Bobby through the air and lumbered after him. Snorting and bucking, the bull's hind feet came down on Bobby's right leg. Scholarship dreams shattered, Bobby turned to his 'wealthy' parents for tuition only to discover they were mortgaged to the hilt and on the verge of bankruptcy.

Bobby focused all his attention on Beth, a vulnerable eighteen-year-old girl with her own ranch. The spoiled jock dated, and then married the only girl Austin ever loved. He was devastated.

It was no surprise when Beth came to Austin's mother for advice. The two had grown close after the girl's mother died. Beth's 'question' was the shocker. Should she sign the ranch over to Bobby? *He* claimed it was only proper now that he was her husband.

"Wait a few years. There's plenty of time," Austin's mother advised with great tact. In private, she told her son, "If she ever puts his name on that deed, he'll sell everything and be long gone."

After that talk, his graceful neighbor became a klutz. Beth's first visible bruise was a black eye. Her story about the bucket falling off the shelf at the exact moment she looked up, just didn't fly with Austin. His gut told him this was the beginning of a bad situation. He was right. Beth wore many bruises over the next four years— too many.

The day Austin dreaded blew in on the heels of a cold, hard winter. It was early May when Beth announced she and Bobby were expecting a baby in December. The bruises stopped. Maybe there was hope after all.

As the sun slithered over the horizon on a cool November evening, Austin stopped in front of Beth's house to let them know their horses were out again. One of these days a car was going to collide with a horse, because Bobby was too lazy to close a gate.

Sobs filled the night air. The front door was open. Beth took a step and collapsed a few feet from him.

"Shut the door. I ain't paying to heat the

whole county," Bobby yelled from his recliner.

"He's drunk again," Beth whispered. Austin ignored the man and helped Beth to her feet. She doubled over in pain. "I can't stand."

Austin swooped her up and carried her to his truck. It was an interminable ride to the hospital. The sight of his passenger brought unbidden tears. Boxers left the ring in better condition.

Unconscious when they reached the hospital, Beth was shifted to a gurney and wheeled into a cubicle in the Emergency Room.

The nervous cowboy tried to sit in a chair, but found himself pacing as the clock on the wall ticked away the seconds.

A nurse approached Austin and asked, "How far along is your wife?"

"No, ma'am, she's my neighbor. I think she's eight months."

With a look of disgust, the nurse turned and marched out of the waiting room. Austin resumed his pacing.

When the nurse finally returned two hours later, Austin believed she had to be the most abrupt person he'd ever met.

"Do you have any idea what happened to her?"

"I can't say for sure. I found her this

way."

"She's awake and asking for Austin. Is that you?"

He nodded.

"We can't stop her labor. That baby is coming tonight." The nurse spoke with a sharp tone and looked repelled by the whole situation. "Follow me." Her suspicious glare left no doubt that she thought he was the one who battered Beth. He followed her down the long hallway to a room where Beth was hooked up to all sorts of monitors and needles. His hand trembled as he removed his Stetson, placed it on a chair and approached the bed.

With a weak smile, she reached for his hand. "I need your help."

"Anything." His voice cracked as he tried to rein in his emotions.

"I don't think I can do this alone, Austin. I know it's asking a lot, but will you stay with me while I have the baby?"

He tried to swallow the lump in his throat. Unable to trust his voice, he squeezed her hand and nodded.

At four in the morning, Austin pushed through the front door of the hospital, exhausted. He marveled at Beth's determination. Because of her condition, the doctor suggested a c-section, but she wanted no part of it. After nine hours of labor, she delivered a beautiful, healthy baby. Bobby's name was never mentioned.

"Daddy, Momma said lunch is ready."

Mollie's voice pulled Austin from the past. The day was speeding by and the work would not do itself. He devoured a quick lunch and then climbed into the cab of the tractor. The sound of the baler chugged behind him as he spent the afternoon making monotonous circles in the field. He would rather be breaking a horse, but Spirit would get his undivided attention tomorrow. Early evening shadows stretched across the front of the barn when he parked the tractor beside the door.

"Daddy, I found some." Mollie ran toward him.

"Some what, honey?"

"Rope."

Not the tire swing again. Hot and tired, he tried to feign interest. "Where did you find it?"

"In that box in the shed. I put it under the tree."

Beads of sweat formed on his forehead, and it wasn't the heat. Mollie had found the rope stashed in the old footlocker. Why hadn't he burned it? Too late now.

"Daddy, are you okay?"

"Just hot. Why don't you run in the house and get me a glass of ice water? I'll put that swing up right now."

He hoisted the step ladder from the barn onto his shoulders and carried it to the old oak. If trees could talk he would have made kindling out of this one long ago.

His mind wandered back to that fateful morning. Driving home from the hospital, he decided to stop and talk with Bobby Jackson. The man should be sober by now.

Austin shook the groggy man in the recliner. "Bobby, wake up. You're a father."

"Huh?" The man rubbed his bloodshot eyes.

"Beth had the baby. It's a girl."

"Just what I need. Another worthless female to feed," Bobby growled.

Austin snapped. He marched out of the house and straight to the barn for the step ladder. He positioned it under a limb of the majestic oak in front of the house. He walked to the truck, opened the glove compartment, and pulled out his pistol, the one he shot mud turtles with the day before.

The steps creaked as Austin entered the house. With the gun aimed at Bobby's head, he said, "Wake up. You've got a letter to write."

Gone was the ex-football star's macho demeanor. His hands trembled as he sat at the table, pen in hand. "I don't know what you want me to write."

"I'm sorry."

Bobby stared at him.

"Just write 'I'm sorry.' That'll be good enough."

They walked to the tree in silence and stopped.

Bobby stared at the tree, the ladder, and the rope hanging from the limb. All remnants of his drunken stupor lifted and he demanded, "Just what are you expecting me to do?"

"The right thing, for once in your miserable life."

For six months, Austin watched Beth struggle with chores. Any spare time he could muster, he helped. The day she said, "We need to talk," his heart sank.

Prepared to hear that she was throwing in the towel, he couldn't believe his ears when she asked him to marry her and adopt Mollie.

"You're so good with the baby and every little girl needs a daddy. I'll give you half the ranch if you'll give us your name. I won't expect you to love me."

"Beth, I don't want your property. All I've ever wanted is you." Tears welled up in the cowboy's eyes. "I'll be proud to give you my name. You already have my heart. I love you and Mollie."

If everyone around hadn't known the abuse Beth suffered, there might have been talk. Instead, they were bombarded with congratulations and good wishes.

Now, seven years later, a tire swing hangs from the oak tree. Someday Mollie will have to be told about her 'real' father. But Austin would never let her, or her mother, find out that Bobby Jackson died from an 'assisted' suicide.

Austin sat on the porch and watched Mollie swing from the same tree as her father. He closed his eyes. Yes, there is more than one way to swing from a tree.

IRRECONCILABLE DIFFERENCES

Henry watched his grandson, David, walk across the gravel road and across the parched yard. A good rain would have helped the grass a week ago, but it was brown and crunchy to the step now.

David stepped onto the porch. "Afternoon, Grandpa."

"Hi, David."

"I guess I need to talk to you," the young man said.

"Nope," Henry stated.

"But Grandpa - -"

"No, David. If you want to talk to me, go get Janie."

"Grandpa, she's busy."

"She's not that busy. If you want to talk to me, go get your wife."

Henry knew his tone was harsh, but the time for polite behavior was over. He had been quiet and kept his opinions to himself. No more. "I'll be waiting in the house." Standing abruptly, he turned and went inside.

Through his front window the older man saw his granddaughter-in-law carry a suitcase to her car. He watched his grandson approach her. Body language spoke volumes. Henry didn't need to hear the conversation to know Janie was less than thrilled to be summoned for a visit. But she would come. His grandson married a sweetheart of a girl. But the girl had married a young man as hard headed as his grandpa. Hard-headed, but not hard hearted. Henry was banking on that.

The young couple crossed the road and crunched across the yard. This was not going to be easy for any of them.

David opened the door. "We're here."

"Come on in. Hi, Janie." Henry took a long look at the couple as David sat in an armchair and Janie took a seat on the couch. "David seems to think we need to talk. So what is going on?"

The young man swallowed hard.

"Grandpa, Janie and I are separating. She is moving home with her parents." He took a deep breath and sat back.

Henry eyed the couple. He studied Janie's face first. Beautiful girl. No. She is a beautiful young woman. Long brown hair. A magnetic, charming, out-going personality. He shifted his gaze to his grandson. Handsome. Stubborn, but fair. He thought they were a perfect match.

"Why are you separating?" He saw no need to tiptoe. He wanted the facts. "David, do you have a girlfriend?"

"Good grief, no!"

"So, Janie, do you have a boyfriend?"

Her face was redder than Rudolph's nose. "Absolutely not!"

"Then what is the problem?"

His grandson stared at him. "It happens, Grandpa. Just call it irreconcilable differences."

"Really?" The older man turned his head toward Janie.

"Yes, Henry," she confirmed. "Irreconcilable differences."

They sat in silence. The only sound was the ticking of the clock on the wall. Henry mulled over this situation. When David and Janie moved to the house in the country, across the road from him, Henry promised his son that he would keep a quiet eye on them. A big city doctor, Henry's son lived hundreds of miles away. He would not have a magic prescription for the problem sitting in his father's living room.

Henry was not sure he could help, but he had to try. "Get up. We're going for a ride."

"Grandpa, I told you Janie is busy," David protested.

"I heard what you said. Now you are going to give me a little time. This is not a request."

Like dutiful children they marched to the car. The fun began. "You can sit in the front seat," David offered to Janie.

"No, thank you. I am used to taking a back seat," Janie snapped.

Henry suspected the girl had a little fire to her but had never witnessed it. He smiled. A good marriage needs spunk.

With David in the front passenger seat and Janie in the back seat, Henry buckled himself behind the wheel.

"Where are we going?"

"You'll see," Henry answered his grandson.

They were on the road less than ten minutes when David asked, "Would you mind if I turned on the radio?"

"Yes."

As David's hand reached for the radio dial, Henry slapped it. "No radio!"

A startled voice snapped, "Grandpa!"

Having never laid a hand on his grandson, Henry winced. Nobody said tough love was easy. Guess that's why they call it tough. "I said no radio. You two need to think."

The next few miles were spent in silence. David moaned when Henry pulled into the cemetery parking lot, but he didn't say a word.

"Get out," Henry ordered.

David and Janie respectfully obeyed, but their expressions displayed confusion. They followed Henry to the tombstone marked "Gloria Pearl Brimer, beloved wife of Henry. December 24, 1950 – April 23, 2015".

"Hey, Pearl. It's me. I brought visitors."

"Grandpa, why did you call her Pearl instead of Gloria?"

"That's easy. She was my precious jewel." Henry looked at Janie. "I wish you had met her. She would have loved you."

David's grandmother passed away three years before they were married, but Janie had heard a lot about her.

Henry pointed at the grave. "That, my dear boy, is separation!"

David bowed his head. Was it shame or reverence? Henry was not sure. Maybe a little of both. "Grandpa, you just don't understand."

"What do you think I can't understand? Do you think I married a grandma?" Henry chuckled. "Pearl was a beautiful, head-strong young lady. Problem was she hitched herself to a mule-headed man."

"You and Grandma argued?" David could not hide his surprise.

"No, we didn't just argue. We fought worse than Democrats and Republicans."

"What about?"

"We were young. We fought about everything. We both had opinions and were convinced we were right."

"But you stayed married? I thought you were happy." David scratched his head.

Janie spoke in a soft tone. "I have heard so many good things about you and your wife. Are you saying they weren't true?"

"Of course they were true. We had a wonderful marriage."

"I'm sorry, Grandpa, but how can you say that if you fought all the time?"

"Because the fighting stopped. At least, we stopped fighting each other." Henry saw the puzzled expressions on David and Janie's faces. "Kids, we stopped fighting each other and started fighting for one another."

"I don't understand," Janie honestly admitted.

"It would have been easy to throw in the towel and walk away. But we vowed 'for better or worse' and we meant it. We decided that when we got angry, we would count to ten and trade places. Try to put ourselves in the other one's shoes. It was time to fight for our marriage."

"Did it work?" David asked.

"It took time. Nothing good happens overnight. What we learned was that many of the arguments we had were nonsense. In the grand scheme of things, who really cares whether the toilet paper goes over or under as long as you have toilet paper?"

Henry looked at the struggling couple. "One would think that this would be called irreconcilable differences." He pointed toward the grave. "One would be wrong." He wiped a tear. "Pearl and I were joined in marriage. Over the years, our hearts got all tangled together. She may be in a different place, but she is always with me. That is what a good marriage is. And it takes work."

David's hand slipped into Janie's. She didn't pull away. They all walked back to the car, but Henry was the only one who took a front seat.

ABOUT THE AUTHOR

Growing up in the Missouri Ozarks, Brenda Brinkley always loved to read and her mother said she had a "wild imagination." Days were spent working outside with dad. At night, mom would find Brenda in the closet with a flashlight reading a book.

Now a wife, mother, grandmother, and great grandma, Brenda still loves to read and write. She has been writing newspaper and magazine articles for over 35 years. Her short stories and photography have won several awards.

Having written for Springfield NewsLeader, Farm Talk Publishing, Ozark's Magazine, Western Mule Magazine, Grit, The Ozark's Mountaineer, and several other publications, Brenda now writes regularly for Ozarks Farm & Neighbor and enjoys meeting all the different farmers who think they are not interesting. Humble folks are truly fascinating people with wonderful stories to tell.

Blessed to be raised in a Christian home, Brenda has a strong faith in God and serves in the church wherever needed.

Brenda also loves to weave rugs, grow and paint gourds, and piece quilts for the grandchildren.